Letting Go

A Novel

By Bill Cronin

Printed in the United States of America.

ISBN: 978-0-9908381-3-5

Library of Congress Cataloging-In-Publication Data
Library of Congress Control Number: 2016910502

Dedication

To my wife Linda, the person I write for.

Special thanks to Wendy Davis, Executive Director, Postpartum Support International, for educating me on the many legal and legislative issues related to Postpartum Psychosis. And to Naomi Knowles, a Postpartum Psychosis survivor, for her personal insights into this dreadful disease.

One

Key West

1996

If a muse were a place, Key West would be mine. If you stripped away the hordes that descended upon the island from cruise-ships, the brashness of Duval Street, the carnival atmosphere on Mallory Square at sunset and those who searched for the hard-drinking ghost of Ernest Hemingway, a quaint island remained, whose laid-back atmosphere inspired creativity like no other place I knew.

Yes, Key West was a harlot. She applied gaudy makeup to appeal to the tourists searching for "Margaritaville" and those who wished to explore the lower keys on their hands and knees. Once she removed her carnival makeup, she was charming, an exceptional beauty and accepting of artists of any creative stripe. Hemingway was emblematic of the Conch Republic. He drank and caroused to excess, but his artistic side enriched people worldwide. Key West inspired me as it had inspired Hemingway to write his most noteworthy novels. In my bleakest hour, when I couldn't write a single sentence, I found my literary footing here. I bound my emotional wounds and stitched together the tattered threads of my life.

My half-sister Billie, her partner, Alexandra and my childhood sweetheart, Jody Holland lived here. I was on the mend, thanks to them. Under the threat of a lawsuit by my ex-publisher, I had returned to Mount Dora and embarked on a writing marathon. I produced two novels in less than three months. In the midst of this herculean effort, my wife of eight years divorced me. When the court had finalized the papers and I had finished the novels, Jody invited me to return to Key West to rest and heal.

It was April and only a faint wisp of spring remained. In just a few weeks, oppressive humidity and heat would return. The snowbirds would withdraw beyond the Mason-Dixon Line. The change in seasons would return control of the Jewel of the Caribbean to the "Conchs," a nickname for those who call Key West home.

Hoping to hit the seven-mile bridge south of Marathon at sunrise, I left Mount Dora by car at two in the morning. I crested the bridge just as the sun breached the horizon and bled out purple, pink and orange on the calm aquamarine waters. At seven-thirty a.m., I called Billie and asked if she, Jody and I could meet at her restaurant at ten thirty for brunch. After I got off the phone, it occurred to me that Billie had always been the arbiter between Jody and me. Billie introduced us when we were fourteen years old. We attended the same swimming and diving classes in Hollywood, Florida. I was too shy to introduce myself to her. Billie mediated. Jody was my first love and the first girl I had ever kissed. Tragedy struck Jody's family and circumstances forced her to move away. After a separation of more than 30 years, Billie brought us together again just a few short months ago.

Seeing Jody was like walking back through a wrinkle in time. Her gracious, calm demeanor remained. She drew me into her warmth as she had so many years ago. When I was with Jody, it was like one continuous emotional embrace. Perhaps it was the softness in her light brown eyes; the way she scoured my face looking for emotional clues. She leaned in close when we talked and she was always touching me. She made every moment feel intimate. As much as I had loved Emily and others before her, I had never felt this way in the presence of anyone else.

"The Mangrove" was Billie's restaurant. On the eastern end of Duval Street near the lighthouse and close to Hemingway's house, it was a courtyard restaurant at the base of two enormous Banyan trees. The boughs of the trees provided shade to the entire property. An older remodeled two-story home housed the kitchen and interior seating. Paved in red used-brick and crammed with round teak tables shaded by green canvas umbrellas, the courtyard was appealing and casual. The bar, a long thin Victorian structure of white painted wood and stained teak, ran the length of the left side of the property. A white picket fence framed the corner lot so that the front and right sides of the courtyard were open to the streets.

I parked my car on Duval Street a few steps from the restaurant. From the host station, at the locked gated entrance, I caught the attention of one of the servers preparing for lunch.

"Hi, I'm Billie's brother. Could you please let her know I'm here?"

I peered over the gate and admired the ambiance of the courtyard as the server disappeared into the main building. The smell of sautéed onions, garlic and peppers filled the air.

"Hey, you," she said, with a tap on my shoulder.

"Hey, you." As I turned to face her, Jody extended her arms around my neck and enveloped me with a hug.

"I've missed you, Jack. I've been counting down the days." She moved away from me enough to kiss me on the cheek.

Jody was tall, athletic, tanned and wore her dirty blond hair straight back into a ponytail. The smile on her lips transmitted what the sunglasses hid – joy. She dressed in white shorts, orange sleeveless top and white, thong sandals.

"I've missed you, too." This time I initiated a hug of my own.

"Ahem." I heard Billie behind me. "Am I interrupting something?"

"I wish you were, Billie," Jody said, laughing, as she pushed away from me to greet Billie.

Billie unlocked the gate, and we took turns giving Billie a hug.

Billie said, "I'm so glad you're both here." To me, she said, "Jack, I'm so sorry about the divorce." To Jody, she said, "I'm amazed you could carve out the time from the gallery. Every time I go by there the place is so busy."

Jody said, "No ships in port. It's a Monday. Duval Street is a ghost town right now. I'll take all the breaks I can get."

"Let's go find a table and lock this gate. I don't want anyone to think we're open."

Billie turned and led us to the main building. Jody slipped an arm through mine as we followed behind. I had never been inside the main building. The front door opened into a foyer of sorts. Straight ahead were Dutch doors that led to a kitchen. To the left were bathrooms, and to the right, where the living room of the house would have been, was the dining room. To the rear, there was a private room. Billie led us to a table next to a picture window that looked out to the courtyard. The room was white, with white painted trim. Framed, colorful Key West scenes lit up the walls. Servers had placed multi-colored gladioli on the tables.

"I made us something special for brunch. I'll put it in the oven." Billie backtracked to the foyer then disappeared into the kitchen.

I pulled Jody's chair out. Once she sat, I slid into the chair next to her.

"I had hoped you would've come sooner. I've been so worried about you, with your father and Aunt Ruby passing away, the divorce, and the mess with your publisher – well – I was just worried."

"I know, Jody, and I appreciate your invitation. If I had come before I finished the last novel, I wouldn't have been able to concentrate. I was making good progress and I needed to keep at it. Now, the pressure is off and you have my full attention."

Jody shifted in her chair to face me. The light from the plate glass window backlighted her hair and her light brown eyes. She put my hand in hers. "How have things gone with Emily? Billie told me you're worried about working with her."

"What did I say?" Billie asked, dressed in black slacks and a black long sleeve blouse. She raked her rusty colored hair with her fingers as she sat down in a huff.

Jody repeated her question for Billie's benefit."

I said, "I think it will work out. She's good at what she does, we work well together and I need her. After my publisher fired me, she and Lisa, my agent, have been searching for another publisher. Working with her is awkward at times, but, so far, we manage." What I hadn't said was the divorce was painful. It had wounded me. I had hoped coming to Key West would aid the healing process.

We caught each other up on events since my last visit. Billie announced a lease burning celebration now that she'd purchased the restaurant with her part of my father's estate. She wanted to wait to schedule the event until I could be there.

"Now that I have the funds, I want to upgrade the kitchen. It's small and out of date. I have a commercial kitchen designer working with my architect and our head chef to create a state-of-the-art facility. I want to elevate food quality and expand our menu to appeal to more sophisticated customers." There was excitement in Billie's tone and her passionate gestures hinted at the love she had for her business.

Jody's gallery, which featured an eclectic mixture of local art, was successful beyond Jody's expectations. She said, "The greatest challenge is keeping high-quality pieces in my gallery. I have a stable of artists who can't keep up with demand. I'm running ads in every town between here and Miami looking for talented artists and craftsman."

"That's a good problem to have, Jody."

Our server brought our food. All three plates were the same.

Billie explained, "This Mexican egg-casserole is a western omelet with a kick." There were three individual servings accompanied by sausage patties and cantaloupe slices cut into the shape of porpoise. The chef had divided the golden-brown crusted casserole into squares. As soon as the server delivered the food, another brought three Bloody Marys. "Something to start the day." Billie raised her glass. "To three healing souls."

While we ate, we chatted about how the cruise ships had changed Key West and brought a more sophisticated tourist to the island. Yes, Key West had a bawdy reputation to maintain, ala Sloppy Joes and The Hogs Breath Saloon. But, the ships brought more upscale patrons to the Southernmost City. They were willing to pay for an upmarket experience and both Jody and Billie hoped to appeal to this class of visitor.

After the second round of Bloody Marys, the servers cleared the dishes from the table. Jody looked at me then Billie. "I want to talk about my mother." Jody's forehead creased, and her shoulders slumped. "She wants to meet in person. I haven't seen her in thirty-five years. She says it is important. She hired a private-detective to track me down, of all things."

I asked her, "Did she call you?"

"An investigator delivered a letter to me three weeks ago. That's when I called you, Jack, about telling my story. To be honest, I've spent a lifetime trying to forget it.

Billie stretched across the table and patted Jody's hand. "What does the letter say, Darlin'?"

Jody pulled out a well-worn folded piece of paper from her shorts and handed it to Billie. After she read it, she passed it to me.

Dearest Jody,

For years, I have been working up the courage to reach out to you. Until now, I have bowed to your need for privacy and your need to forget about what happened. I just turned seventy-three. It occurred to me that opportunities to tell you how sorry I am face to face are dwindling. What I put you through and the trauma you suffered at my hand are unforgivable. Given the circumstances, I expect you to be skeptical of my expressions of love, which are true and deep. There is another side to the horror of our story, an explanation of how and why it happened. I would like the opportunity to tell you my side of the story before the opportunity is gone forever.

I would like to come see you. I would completely understand if you declined or don't respond. I think, though, what I have to share with you will sharpen your understanding of what happened and why. I suspect that, deep down, you may want to know—at least I pray that's the case.

She signed it, "Helen." Below her signature were Helen's address and telephone number.

I folded up the fatigued paper and gave it back to Jody. "Are you going to meet with her?"

Jody moved the note from one hand to the other and then laid it on the table in front of her. "I don't know. She's right about one thing. There is much I don't know. First, my family protected me from any news about my mother. Then, I tried to bury it with drugs and alcohol. When I was in counseling, information about what happened could only come from my mother. I had no idea of where she was and I had no desire to dig it all up again."

I asked her, "How can I help?"

Jody reached out to me and took my hand in hers again. "I want you to help me find out what happened, Jack. I don't want to do it alone."

"Of course."

"I want to know what I'm getting myself in for before I agree to meet with my mother."

"I understand, Jody."

"Then you will help?"

"Yes, of course."

Billie said, "Jody, digging around in family closets can be painful. You sure you want that?"

"That's exactly why I want Jack's help. I'm not strong enough to face this alone. But I need to confront it. This is an open wound in my life that needs to heal."

Two

Hollywood, Florida

July 1961

At 5:30 a.m., Mario Moretti couldn't sleep. The FBI had been investigating the Hollywood Police Department for corruption. Mario's Italian heritage and previous employment history with the New York Police Department, known for corruption issues of its own, made him an easy target for investigators. He was clean, but he understood why he was under suspicion. While Mario felt the PD command staff was above corruption, he knew many of the cops he worked with were not.

Kathy, his wife of twenty years, got out of bed, reached for a robe, slipped her arms in and straightened the thin garment around her.

"You're wide awake."

He said, "The FBI thing."

The day prior, an FBI agent cornered him at a local burger joint and threatened to subpoena him if he didn't cooperate with their investigation.

"What're you going to tell them?"

"No matter what I say, I'm screwed."

"Tell them you're clean, and that you refuse to comment on anything else."

"If I say that, I'm admitting that the department is on the take. Then they'll crush me to tell them what I know. If I refuse to tell them anything, then they'll assume that I'm dirty, too."

"Take your shower, and I'll fix some coffee. We'll figure something out," Kathy said over her shoulder as she aimed for the kitchen.

As Mario pulled clean underwear from his dresser, the phone in the kitchen rang. He sat on the mattress knowing the call was from the PD; no one else would call at this hour.

"It's the chief. He says it's urgent," Kathy stood at the doorway.

"Is he still on the phone?" He turned around to see the expression on her face. Kathy was forty-four and Mario thought she was still as attractive as the day he married her. Her braided black hair hung down to her waist and her narrow thin face showed concern.

"No. He just asked that you come to a crime scene immediately. I wrote down the address."

"Did he say what it's about?"

"Nope. He didn't sound good, though. Not his business-as-usual manner. He sounded upset. You get your shower, and I'll make some coffee."

Mario scrambled to get dressed. "No time. I'll get some coffee from the donut shop on Johnson Street later."

Kathy moved to her side of the bed and sat down. "You don't think the subpoena threat could be a fishing expedition do you? A way to sweat you for information."

Mario considered it. "I hadn't thought about that. I wouldn't put it past them."

"Then I wouldn't worry about it until you get served some paper. You don't have anything to worry about do you?"

Mario looked at her. The Italian evil eye, Kathy liked to call it.

"Well that came out wrong. That's not what I meant. I'm sorry. You know how cops are. When they go down the toilet, they like to flush everyone with them. I just don't want you caught in someone else's backwash."

Kathy had been a dispatcher on the job with him in NY. She'd witnessed corruption inquisitions launched by NYPD Internal Affairs. She knew, when the shit hit the fan in corruption sweeps, everyone caught their share.

"I'm good, Kathy. I wouldn't jeopardize what we have over a few lousy bucks."

"Aren't you at least going to shave?"

"I'll use the electric razor at work. This sounds pretty urgent."

Mario kissed Kathy, bent down and hugged her.

She said, "Don't forget Clarissa's birthday. Dinner and party at six-thirty."

"They grow up so fast." Mario couldn't believe Clarissa was fourteen today. "Before you know it all four of them will be grown up and on their own. Sorry to run."

"I know."

Due to the insane hours he worked, the chief had assigned Mario a city cruiser he drove home at night. When he got in the car, he flipped on the Motorola police-band radio mounted under the dash. All he heard were multiple ambulances dispatched to Pierce Street, the location Kathy had given him.

"What the hell's going on?" he said to himself.

When Mario turned onto Pierce Street, between the ocean and the Intracoastal Waterway, emergency lights from half the cars in the department washed every surface in red. Several ambulances helped to make the street impassable. Homes around the scene were lit up and residents huddled together at the curb observing the melee. Mario parked on the side of the road behind the chief's car and jogged to the subject house. As he approached the front door, a patrol officer bolted out and puked into the hedges. As Mario walked in, he met the chief as he came out.

"Phil, what's going on?"

Ignoring his question Chief Thompson said, "Good, you're here. I want you to take a look at this."

Mario followed the aging chief into the home. Lying face down, just inside the door, was a man dressed only in his underwear. Blood was draining from a wound in the middle of his forehead. Behind him, another patrol officer had placed a small, frail woman—in her late thirties—in handcuffs. A girl, Clarissa's age, stood behind her suffering from a wound to the right side of her head. Blood covered her pajamas, but she appeared to be all right. The woman in cuffs kept saying, "Oh God what have I done? I killed them. I killed them all."

Chief Thompson looked at Mario and said, "This is just the beginning. Come with me." He followed Thompson to the back of the house and turned into one room where medics had loaded the body of an infant girl onto a backboard. She'd been shot in the temple from what looked like a small caliber weapon. The smell of gunpowder filled the room.

There was a crib, from which the attendants had just removed the infant child, and two other twin beds occupied by children both of whom had been shot in the head. One boy about three or four and another older male about seven or eight lay on their beds in a pool of blood. One of the medical technicians said, referring to the infant, "She still has a pulse."

Another attendant huddled over the younger boy and said, "I don't know how, but this boy is still alive, too."

Phil walked over to the older boy, felt for a pulse at the neck and shook his head. "Let's get these kids to the hospital ASAP."

To Mario the chief said, "We aren't done." Phil led Mario out of the room as medics raced the surviving children to awaiting ambulances. In the next room, a female child lay on the floor with a gunshot wound to the temple. Attendants lifted a girl onto a gurney and covered the child's face. Blood covered both beds. The other bed must have belonged to the surviving girl.

"Find out what happened here, Mario. Drop everything you're doing. You're lead on this." The chief pulled a handkerchief from his pocket and wiped his eyes. "Sometimes I hate this job."

Mario followed the chief out of the bedroom and back to the living room where the handcuffed woman sat on the couch. "Mario, interview the girl while things are still fresh, then get her off to the hospital. Make sure the Identification Bureau scours the crime scene. Keep me posted." The chief left him standing in the living room. A medic bandaged the head of the older girl while the woman sat on the couch repeating that she'd 'killed them all.'

The child cried. Blood matted her blond hair. Blood and tears covered the right side of her face. Still standing, she rocked back and forth on bare feet. All Mario could think about was Clarissa as he watched the medic clean the wound above her ear. The attendant dashed into the kitchen, returned with a wet washcloth and cleaned her face. The young girl stared at him, still producing tears faster than the medic could wipe them away. Mario took a handkerchief from his pocket, handed it to the girl and she leapt into his arms and sobbed. He just held her and rocked her back and forth.

Mario told the patrol officer standing next to the handcuffed woman to take her to the station. That he would be there soon.

He looked down at the girl's bandaged head buried in his chest. "Come with me, sweetheart." He considered going out the front door, but thought better of parading the girl before gawkers on the street. The Florida room was empty of any evidence of carnage. Mario led the girl to a small wicker couch with green and red floral cushions. He eased her into a sitting position then sat next to her. She was taller than Clarissa but the same age. He wondered if they went to school together. He could see a crucifix hanging from the wall in the living room. They appeared to be Catholic, and Clarissa went to Little Flower School, a Catholic elementary school in town not far from the crime scene.

The girl sat with her hands in her lap, her head down and still crying. "What is your name, sweetheart?"

"Jody," she said without lifting her head.

Mario slipped his forefinger under her chin and lifted her face up. Her eyes were light brown. Her face tanned and her hair sun-bleached. The bandage the medic had wrapped around her forehead and ear stemmed the flow of blood. He wiped the tears from her cheeks. "Jody, I know this is hard, but can you tell me what happened?"

She sniffed back a runny nose. "I was asleep and heard this bang and then another right next to me but I couldn't wake up." Her eyes welled up, her mouth contorted and her shoulders heaved.

He hugged her and told her it would be okay, knowing it wouldn't. She regained a modicum of composure. "I kept hearing more explosions. When I woke up, I was bleeding and I saw Jeannie on the floor. There was blood everywhere. I ran to get my mom. Dad was lying on the living room floor and I found Mom sitting on the floor in their bedroom trying to put bullets in the gun. She'd shot everyone!" She looked up at me. "She told me, 'Go call the police.' I called the operator and asked her to call the police. Then I took the gun away from her. She was trying to kill herself! I put the gun on their dresser and just held her until the police came." She wiped her eyes again. "She tried to kill me!" She looked at me, then into the living room as medics loaded her father onto a gurney and removed the last body from the house.

Mario signaled for one of the patrol officers. "Call the station. Have Rodriguez get over here on the double. I want her to escort Jody to the hospital. And clear the crowd away from the front of the house. I want to take the girl out of here and I don't want a circus."

The girl asked Mario, "Can't you stay with me?"

"Jody, sweetheart, the doctors need to take a look at that wound on your head. You need stitches and I need to look after things here. Officer Rodriguez is a nice woman. She'll take good care of you. Would that be all right with you?"

She nodded.

"Do you have any family here in Hollywood?"

"No. My Grammy and Poppy went back to Pennsylvania a couple of weeks ago. My aunt lives in Atlanta."

Mario got their names and he wrote them in his notebook. He escorted the girl through the house and out the front door. Officers had moved the curious back down the street behind barricades. He led Jody to Sergeant Rodriguez's pool car. The sergeant, who headed the dispatch unit, introduced herself to Jody, gave her a hug and opened the passenger door.

"After you take her to the hospital," he tore a page from his notebook and handed it to Rodriguez, "I want you to call her aunt and grandparents and let them know what happened. Make sure someone stays with the girl until she has family with her."

Mario, put his hand through the passenger window and touched Jody's cheek. "Doris will take you to the hospital and I'll be by to see you later to make sure you're okay."

Jody nodded, her cheeks still wet with tears. He watched her as the car pulled away. The sun broke on the horizon. Humidity clung to his skin in beads. A breeze blew off the ocean, a half a block away, as though this day were no different from the millions of days that had preceded it. As Mario watched the car stop and turn left on A1A, he knew this horrific day would change Jody's life in ways no one could predict.

Three

Hollywood

1961

Mario stepped back toward the Holland home. The Identification Bureau had arrived and unpacked their equipment. Dressed in street clothes, their first step was to rope off the yard. The street dead-ended at the Broad Walk, a macadam strip that separated the beach sand from the homes and businesses that abutted it. To the west, at Mario's instruction, barricades blocked vehicular and pedestrian traffic several doors down from the Holland's home. The scene was secure.

To John Williams, the technician-in-charge, a short heavy set black man, Mario said, "Get a hold of yourself before you go in there." Even though medics had removed the bodies, the scene was gruesome.

Once in the house, Mario retraced his steps. From the blood patterns on the pillows and crib, Mrs. Holland had shot each of her children at close range in the head. The second oldest girl had crawled from the bed after her mother shot her and succumbed to her injuries on the floor.

From the position of the husband on the living room floor, the gunshots had awakened him and he came to investigate. Mrs. Holland intercepted her husband in the living room and shot him in the head.

In the master bedroom, the .22 caliber revolver Jody had wrestled from her mother lay on top of the dresser as she'd reported. Where Jody had said her mother had attempted to reload the handgun, an empty cartridge box lay on its side; .22 caliber shells covered the floor.

To the ID Unit, he pointed out the location of the father, and the second oldest daughter both found on the floor, and then the location of the other victims. "Find the six slugs and casings, John. Take plenty of pictures." Williams was as thorough a crime scene investigator as anyone from the NYPD. Meticulous, competent, patient and organized, he commanded the quiet respect of his team. "There is little doubt what happened. How it happened and why, those are the real questions," Mario said to Williams. "And when you're done, tag and bag the sheets and transport them to the coroner's office so that positive blood matches can be made." Although there were two children still alive when medics transported them to the hospital, Mario knew their gunshot wounds were so severe they wouldn't survive.

Satisfied Williams had the crime scene under control, Mario walked from the Holland home to his car. Except for his vehicle and the ID unit's van, all emergency vehicles, save one patrol car, had left the scene. One officer remained to keep on-lookers away. He opened the door, sat behind the wheel and took a deep breath. The horror of what he'd just witnessed consumed him. "Lord, Jesus," he said and tried to remove the pictures of each of the blood-splattered children from his mind. "How could a mother do this to her children? How could she perform such a monstrous act?" he asked himself. The parallels between this family and his were stark. They were both apparently Catholic. He had four children under fourteen, the Hollands, five. Kathy and the woman they hauled off in cuffs were close in age. That this could happen to such innocent children was beyond Mario's experience.

Senseless violence had surrounded his childhood in Brooklyn. As an NYPD cop, gruesome murders had hardened him. By the time he'd made detective and began to investigate the murders that plagued the city, seeing dead bodies murdered in every conceivable fashion, was commonplace. Nothing in his past, nothing in this job or any other job he'd had in law enforcement, had prepared him for what he'd seen this morning. Nothing! All he thought about was his own children and how he would have felt if this had happened to them. He wrestled with his emotions. He pulled out his note pad and made detailed notes on the crime scene and other details that came to mind that he would need when he questioned the suspect.

Mario radioed ahead to have Mrs. Holland placed in an interrogation room. On his way in, he stopped at a donut shop for coffee, passing on food. At the station, several of the officers who were at the scene, huddled around the desk sergeant each sharing what they had seen and heard. He made his way to his desk in the detective bureau bullpen and asked bureau secretary, Mable McBride, to bring a recorder and steno pad with her and follow him to the interrogation room. When they entered the room, a uniformed officer stood guard and Mrs. Holland was still in restraints. She looked bird frail. There was no expression on her face. She sat quietly, eyes fixed on the blank grey wall in front of her.

To the officer, Mario said, "Why don't you wait outside. We can take it from here."

Constructed with soundproofing, the walls were painted battleship gray. Except for glass in the door, the room was windowless. A gray military surplus table and four chairs filled the space. The white linoleum tile was permanently soiled. A fluorescent light mounted to the cracked plastered ceiling added to the room's harsh appearance.

Helen Holland sat with her hands in her lap, with her back against the chair. Her face was expressionless. She hadn't moved since Mario came into the room. McBride placed the reel-to-reel recorder in the middle of the table and plugged it into a nearby receptacle. She placed a fresh tape on one reel, fished the new tape through the recording head and then strung the magnetic tape around the empty reel. She plugged a microphone into the machine and placed it in front of the suspect. She took a seat opposite Mrs. Holland, placed a spiral steno pad in front of her. Mario took a seat next to McBride. He thought Holland's eyes looked dead and black as charcoal. Mario signaled to McBride with a nod to turn on the recorder.

"For the record, the following statement is given by Helen Holland to detective Mario Moretti and police secretary Mable McBride on July 21, 1961 at," Mario looked at his watch, "eight a.m." McBride used shorthand to document the interview.

"Mrs. Holland, I'm Detective Mario Moretti of the Hollywood Police Department. This is Mrs. McBride. It is my duty to advise you of the seriousness of this case, and to question you about the events this morning. Before asking you any questions, I want to advise you that you may first consult with an attorney before you say anything. I also want to advise you that whatever you say may be held for or against you in a court of law. You don't have to tell me anything. Do you understand this?"

"Yes."

"What is your full name?"

"Helen Marie Holland."

"How old are you?"

"Thirty-eight."

"Where do you live?"

She gave Mario the correct address.

"Mrs. Holland, for the record would you describe for us what you did this morning?"

"I killed them all."

"By all, who do you mean?"

"My children and my husband."

"Do you believe that what you did was wrong?"

"Oh, yes. I know it was wrong. But, I didn't have a choice."

"Would you say that what you did was morally wrong?"

"Legally and morally wrong," she said.

"When did the thought of doing this first enter your mind?"

"A couple of weeks ago."

"Did you think how you were going to do it?"

"Yes, there was only one way."

"And what was that?"

"The gun."

"Let's go back to earlier this morning when this happened. Approximately what time was it when you decided that you were going to kill your family?"

"I've been trying for maybe two or three weeks."

"You kept thinking about it?"

"Yes."

"What time this morning did you finally decide that you were going to do it?"

"I've been trying to decide, and then I said, "I can't do it. I can't do it."

"What time was it when you fired the first shot?"

"I don't know. It must have been close to five-thirty."

"At five-thirty this morning?"

"Yes."

"Had you slept at all?"

"No, not really. I don't sleep very much."

"Alright. Now, tell us what you did when you got up this morning. Tell us, step by step, exactly what happened."

"When I woke up, I laid there for a while thinking. My thoughts always came back that we can't go back and we can't go forward. We just don't belong here. We can't go on this way. The children don't have a mother or father. I can't take care of them. God won't take me back and let me live my life over again. I thought of Hell, like I always have. I thought, "Oh God, I can't go to Hell," but I know we're going to Hell. They can't live any longer. We just can't go on like this. It's been the same way every morning. Every morning, every morning, every day, every day and every night; and then I got up and smoked a couple of cigarettes and paced up and down the kitchen like I always do. I went in there and got the gun, and I put it under Jody's bed. Then I thought some more and smoked another cigarette and then went back and stood over her for a long time and said, "I can't, I can't, I just can't. And I said, "You have to. You're going to Hell anyway.

23

You can't do anything about these kids anyway. They're all sick. They have no mother or father the way they should have. Thomas was a good father, but it takes a mother. And then, I just stood over her and over her again. I don't know how I pulled the trigger. I just don't know how. But I did. I know I did. And then, I said, "Oh God, Oh God" and I went around and killed Michael, Jeannie, Daniele and then the baby. And Thomas came running into the living room and I shot him. And I went into our bedroom and Jody came in. I thought she was dead, but anyway I tried to load the gun again, but the shells wouldn't go in. Something on the gun was jammed. Then I told her to call the police. I tried to load the gun again, but Jody grabbed it from me. Then the police came. That's all, I guess, but I'm sane."

Mario couldn't believe this diminutive woman recounted such a heinous crime without a shred of emotion. She spoke as matter-of-factly as one would describe rising in the morning, reading the morning newspaper and then going for a stroll. She sat with her hands folded in her lap.

"Mrs. Holland, just for the record, which one of your children did you shoot first?"

"Jody."

"How old is Jody?"

"Fourteen."

"The second?"

"In the order of their ages."

"I'm sorry?"

"I shot them from the oldest to the youngest."

"From the oldest to the youngest?"

"Yes."

"You said you went and got the gun. Where was the gun?"

"On the shelf in the closet of our room."

"The master bedroom?"

"Yes."

"And the bullets, they were there, too?"

"Yes, in a box with the gun."

"And whose gun was it?"

"My husband's."

"Where did you sleep last night?"

"Things have been a little messed up since I came home from the hospital. I slept in the baby's room."

"Hospital?"

"Yes, I was in the hospital for a couple of months."

"Why were you in the hospital?"

"I'm dead inside. I have no emotions."

"When did you begin to feel this way?"

"After I had the baby."

Mario looked down at his notes, "Robert?"

"Yes, when I came home I just wasn't right. I just couldn't manage. I couldn't sleep. I went back to the doctor that delivered the baby and he said I had a bad case of the baby-blues and sent me to some jerk psychiatrist. And he put me in the hospital."

"And how long were you in the hospital?"

"Twice."

"Twice?"

"The first time was for a few days. They said I needed to rest. But I knew I wasn't right. I was afraid to touch the baby. Afraid that I would hurt him."

"And who was the doctor that put you in the hospital?"

"Dunfree, in Fort Lauderdale."

"And what happened when you got out of the hospital the first time?"

"I tried to kill myself."

"Why?"

"I felt dead. I knew God hated me. I hated me. I was a horrible mother. I didn't want my baby or to be around anyone."

"Did you have thoughts of killing your family then?"

"Yes, but I couldn't do it. I just couldn't."

"How did you try to kill yourself?"

"I took some pills. But I couldn't even do that right."

Mario had interrogated murders of every description; they were all crazy to some extent. But it wasn't his job to make a determination of sanity. As obvious as her poor mental state was, his job was to get the facts, charge the defendant and, in the case of felony murder, turn the case over to the State Attorney for prosecution.

Mario asked her, "Did you ever try to talk with your husband about how you were feeling?"

"No, no one understood. Not even him. I had no feelings, no emotions. I can't talk to anyone about this because it doesn't make sense to anybody but me, and I'm not crazy. Nobody can understand."

"Do you have any remorse?"

"No. I have no feelings. I lost them a long time ago. I just know it was wrong."

"When did you lose your feelings?"

"When the baby was born."

"Are you sorry you did it?"

"I wish I hadn't, yes. But we couldn't go on. I just wish that Jody hadn't taken the gun from me."

"Why do you say that?"

"I wanted to kill myself. That's the only way we could all be together."

"How many bullets were in the gun?"

"Six or so, I guess."

"Did you load the gun yourself?"

"Yes."

"Where did you shoot the children, what parts of their body?"

"In the head."

"Why did you choose the head rather than some other part?"

"So they wouldn't suffer."

"How old were your children, Mrs. Holland?

"Fourteen, ten, eight, four and five months."

"And your husband, how old was he?"

"Forty-two."

"Mrs. Holland, why did you feel it necessary to kill your family?"

"We just couldn't live anymore."

"Why?"

"Because I couldn't be a mother. I couldn't take care of them. I'm a terrible mother."

"What made you think that?"

"Cause I have no emotions. I lost the children a long, long time ago."

"They were good children weren't they?"

"No, but it wasn't their fault. It was my fault because they didn't have a mother. I wanted to love them, but I couldn't."

"When did you stop loving them?"

"Now that I look back, I guess I never loved them, but I thought I did."

"Even that tiny five month old baby?"

"Yes, I'm dead inside."

"When did you first feel that none of you could go on living?"

"I've been thinking of it for the last month. I couldn't go and leave them here."

"You mean you couldn't commit suicide and leave them behind?"

"Yes. Since the baby was born, I was just not right. I knew that when I came out of delivery. I didn't want my baby, and didn't want to be with him. I had thoughts of dropping the baby out the window. I saw myself throwing him out the window of the hospital. I knew I was a horrible mother to think those things and didn't deserve to be a mother. It wasn't the children's fault they had no mother and no father. We just couldn't go on that way. So I tried to kill myself."

"Did you tell anyone that you wanted to kill your baby?"

"No, if I told them, they would take my babies away. I couldn't trust anyone. They would hurt my children. I couldn't let that happen."

"Did you want to kill your family, Mrs. Holland?"

"No, but I had no choice."

"Why did you feel you didn't have a choice?"

"I couldn't take care of them. No one could take care of them. We were going to Hell if I didn't do something. I couldn't leave them behind. I had to take them with me. We just couldn't go on the way it was."

"Is there anything you would like to say before we conclude this interview?"

"No."

"Has anyone mistreated you in any way?"

"I don't understand why everyone is trying to be so nice to me after what I did."

"For the record, this interview was concluded at . . .," he looked at his wristwatch, ". . . eight-twenty a.m."

Mario looked at McBride and signaled her to turn off the recorder.

"Mrs. Holland, I'm going to charge you with the murders of your family, and the attempted murder of your daughter, Jody. Do you understand?"

"Yes," she said without reaction.

"You will remain in the holding cell for a few hours until we can complete our paperwork. Then we will transfer you to the Broward County Jail. The State Attorney's office in Fort Lauderdale will handle your case after that. Do you have any questions?"

She shook her head.

"I'll have an officer come and escort you."

Mario opened the door and asked the officer to take Holland to a cell.

When the officer and Holland left the room Mario sat across from McBride, "What are your thoughts, McBride?"

"She's obviously sick."

"Anyone who deliberately shoots another is sick in my book, McBride. She planned the murders and she knew what she was doing. She even admitted it was wrong. This is no crime of passion. These were cold-blooded and calculated murders. She planned every detail; even killed those children in birth order. You should have seen those kids, McBride. It makes me sick to my stomach." Mario pushed himself away from the table, stood and began to pace the small, square room. "And she sits there," he points at her empty chair, "cool as a scotch on the rocks, not a stitch of remorse and says 'she's dead inside.' That little bitch took five innocent lives this morning. Five!" Mario couldn't erase the picture of the infant shot in the temple. "It was a massacre. And, the oldest girl? The irony is that the Holland bitch shoots her oldest girl and then the girl saves her life! The only good to come out of this is I'll get to see this monster fried in the electric chair."

Mario looked down at McBride and realized that the intensity of his anger had made her feel uncomfortable.

He didn't care. He said. "I called the Sheriff's office earlier and asked them to assign a detective to the crime scene. Call the Sheriff's office and find out whom they've assigned, I want them to meet me at the Sheriff's office. Then call the State Attorney and try to get an appointment with Jonathan Richter after lunch. If they haven't heard what's going on, fill them in. Warn them about the press. And before you do anything, get Holland's shrink on the line. I want to talk with him as soon as you can arrange it."

"Alright. Anything else?"

"I'm worried about the girl, Jody. Call Rodriguez. I want to know that the Holland kid has family with her. What a nightmare for her. Post two officers at the hospital entrance with instructions to keep reporters outside. I don't want the press anywhere near that kid. Call the administrator of the hospital and make sure they're prepared for the press onslaught."

"Anything else."

"Pray for that little girl in Hollywood Hospital. She needs all the help she can get. Find out if I can stop and see her after I talk to the shrink."

Four

The Mangrove Restaurant

Key West 1996

Jody's face wore the stress of the letter from her mother. She looked tired, defeated and frayed. Billie had disappeared into the kitchen to prepare to open the restaurant at eleven-thirty.

I said, "Jody, let's take a walk down to Mallory Square."

She nodded. As we stood up to leave, I looked around for Billie. We stopped at the café door to the kitchen and Billie stood with the chef going over something. I caught her eye, signaled that we were leaving. She waved and went back to her discussion.

Duval Street came to life. Shop owners pulled racks of clothing, trinkets and merchandise onto the sidewalk as Hemingway might cast bait into the ocean in search of the great Marlin. Some swept the sidewalks, while window washers moved from store to store washing ocean salt from the glass. Even at eleven-thirty in the morning, revelers filled Sloppy Joe's to capacity and their jukebox blasted Reggae music onto the streets.

As we walked, I asked Jody what she remembered about her mother and what had happened. I reached for her hand and she clasped it.

"Before Robert was born, my mother was upbeat, happy and carefree. If she had bouts with depression, I never saw them. When she had Robert, something happened. She was like two different people. One day she seemed so normal and the next, she didn't want the baby. She didn't want to be with anyone."

"When I met her, she seemed to be most gracious. I liked her."

"I know, Jack. About a week after the baby was born, Dad took her back to her doctor. At first, Dad wouldn't talk to me about what was going on with Mom. He would just say that she wasn't feeling well. The doctor put her into the hospital to rest; that's what my dad told me anyway. She was there for a few days. When she came home, she seemed to be worse. She closed the door to her room and spent days behind a locked door. We had to put Robert on formula because Mom didn't want to feed him; didn't want to be around him. She went back into the hospital again, this time for two months. Dad took me out of school to help him take care of the kids, but I couldn't handle it. Jeannie was running through the house and fell into a marble windowsill. Since I didn't drive, I couldn't take her to the hospital. That was the final straw. Dad brought Mom home from the hospital again. She'd only been home a week when you met her. When she first came home, she seemed like her old self again. But after you met her she started to decline again. Dad described her as depressed and asked me not to talk to anyone about it."

We walked past Hard Rock Café, then Planet Hollywood and then to the base of Duval Street. We turned left, angled our way past several buildings and found a bench in the shade of a tree on Mallory Square.

"What was wrong with her?" We sat on the bench, facing each other.

"All Dad would say was that she was depressed. It is obvious she had some sort of mental problem."

"What can you recall from that morning?"

"That's what's strange. I don't remember anything and I have tried, Jack. The only memories I have are when you and the detective came to visit me in the hospital. I remember the detective, his face, but I don't remember our conversation except for him telling me that I would see you again. And I remember the doctors telling me that my family had all died except for Mom, of course."

"Do you remember telling me what happened?" I can still remember her giving me a detailed rundown of the events of that morning. How she got up, found her brothers and sisters shot, her father shot and her mother trying to reload the gun to kill herself.

"I remember being in the hospital and asking for you. I remember you coming and you held me. But, no, I don't remember any of it. If you remember me telling you what happened, it's obvious that I've suppressed those memories."

"Who could blame you, Jody?"

She reached for my hand. "How could a woman, I don't care how sick she was, how could she shoot her entire family? How could she shoot those little babies?" She began to cry.

I moved closer to console her.

"I'm concerned about seeing her. I still have deep wounds from it. I'm still so angry at her and words fail to describe how deep that loathing is." She turned toward me, buried her face into my shoulder and continued to cry.

After a few moments, she pulled away, looked at me and said, "What could she tell me that would change how I feel about her? How could I forgive her for what she did to my family, what she tried to do to me?" She looked away, out to the multi-million dollar homes under construction on Tank Island, recently renamed "Sunset Key." "I've prayed that this day would never come."

"So don't meet with her."

"I don't want to," she said, looking back at me – the sun catching her light brown eyes. "But she said she has information, Jack."

"Now it's my turn to be skeptical. What information could she share that would alter what she did, Jody?"

"I agree. But there is one burning question that hasn't let me rest. Why? Why did she do it?"

"She was crazy."

"That doesn't answer my question."

"If you knew the answer to that question, would you welcome your mother back into your life?"

"No! Understanding doesn't equal forgiveness. I could never forgive her. Never."

"Then why is 'knowing why' so important?"

"My father, brothers and sisters are all buried in a cemetery in Hollywood. My siblings never had a chance. I can't help thinking about Robert . . . five-month-old Robert . . . what a senseless act. There was a reason this happened. Their lost lives have to mean more than some senseless, random act of violence. There has to be more to it than that."

"What if there isn't." I asked, trying to lower her expectations. I was convinced at this point that she'd already made up her mind to push forward.

"This still haunts me, Jack."

"When I think about it, Jody, it haunts me, too."

"You went through it with me."

"They were indelible events for both of us. We were both dealing with incredible stress. We were kids faced with adult problems. I had just learned that Billie was my sister and that Mother and Father had hidden her existence from me. You were dealing with the extraordinary pressure of trying to be a mother to your siblings. We were both so needy. Then there was the horror of what happened to your family. Then your aunt ripped you away from me."

Jody said, "I remember sitting on the beach pouring out my heart to you. We talked about deep things and drew strength from each other. I have never felt that connection with another living soul."

"Me neither, Jody."

"Jack, I want to be with you now more than ever. It isn't just the sex, although that would be nice. If I could crawl inside you, I would do it just to be closer to you. I need you to hold me. Do you understand?"

I did. Jody and I had come to this point twice since we reconnected a few months ago. On both previous occasions, I was still married to Em; I was still trying to reconcile my marriage. Despite my best efforts, Em was adamant about the divorce, a divorce that became final several weeks ago. I hadn't been in a position to act on my feelings for Jody. I was somewhat reluctant to take our relationship to a physical level because I still had feelings for Em, and I struggled now with those feelings. I felt like I would be cheating on Emily despite the fact that she made it clear that she no longer wanted me. Complicating it was my continuing work relationship with Em, the feeling that I didn't want Em to know about Jody. I knew these thoughts were not rational, but those feelings were nibbling at the edges of my reality.

At the same time, my feelings for Jody mirrored the feelings she'd expressed. I wanted to be with her. I needed the closeness that she offered. In a way, we were both at the same point we had been as kids. Both of us were facing stressful circumstances. Both of us needed comfort and emotional support. Both of us needed to explore each other's deep feelings and emotions, to work through them and to heal. Although I still had feelings of guilt, I decided to set them aside for now and the last of my reservations fell away.

We walked along the waterfront holding hands. We found our way to the Pier House Havana Docks, their version of a sunset deck, ordered Margaritas and enjoyed the sun and warm temperatures. We spent the afternoon catching up.

The waiter refreshed our drinks. Sailboats crisscrossed in front of the Pier and pelicans, perched on old pilings, ignored them. The smell of food cooking at the Pier House, salt from the ocean and diesel fuel from the sailboats chugging along with sails furled, filled the air.

Jody finally asked me again about Emily.

"What would you like to know?"

"How are you feeling about the divorce?"

"Like I failed. I don't like the person I was, the person that caused Emily to want to leave me. It wasn't her fault. I let her down."

"You were sick, Jack. How is that your fault?"

I had a hard time squaring this line of logic. "It was my fault."

"Did you choose depression, Jack?"

"Of course not."

"Did you choose to hurt Emily?"

"No."

"Then how is this your fault?"

"I have to take responsibility for what I did."

"You put your life back together. She was not willing to wait for you to work through it. 'In sickness and in health.' Who didn't live up to that commitment, Jack?"

I was silent as I considered what she'd just said.

"You tried to work it out. You may regret that it happened, but you're not to blame."

More silence. I may have understood what she was saying with my head, but my heart was another matter.

She asked, "Are you still in love with her?"

"Do you want honesty?"

She nodded.

"Yes." A part of me will always love her, I said to myself. I had to be honest. I didn't want to hold anything in reserve. "If she'd been willing to work things out I would have stayed with her. The commitment I made to her meant something to me. And I'm grieving the loss of that relationship."

"Will those feelings interfere with us?"

"No, Jody. I wouldn't have come down here to be with you without having resolved that."

"What if she changes her mind?"

"She won't, Jody."

"Jack, this is important to me. If she were to change her mind and want you back, what would you do?"

"I'm done with Emily, Jody. Yes, I still care for her. Yes, I'm still hurting from how it all ended. But I'm beyond going back. I'm not going back."

"Even if she were to stand here today and tell you that she loves you and has changed her mind?"

"No, I wouldn't go back to her."

"I have your word?"

"Yes."

Jody stared at me processing what I told her. "Then I won't ask you again about this."

Tourists and locals filled the Havana Docks to enjoy the ritual of happy hour and the setting sun. As sunset approached, we left the Pier House and followed the crowds to Mallory Square. Street performers jockeyed for position and hawked their shows competing with each other for tips from the crowd. As patrons filled the square, it was difficult to hear Jody over the din of conversations, laughter and the increasing volume of live music around us. We abandoned the square in favor of a small Italian restaurant on Duval Street where we had dinner and then went to Jody's cracker-style home on Simonton Street. On two occasions, we'd stood on the porch to her home and I declined her invitation to stay the night. That night, I did not.

Five

Hollywood, Florida

July 1961

Mario Moretti introduced himself to the receptionist at the office of Dr. James Dunfree. She showed him to a conference room off the small reception area. Dunfree sat with a file opened in front of him. He was a thin man in his late-thirties with graying hair at the temples and a long thin clean-shaven face.

Mario introduced himself, they shook hands and he sat at the table opposite the doctor.

"Did the secretary at the police department explain why I'm here to see you?"

"Yes, she did."

"What can you tell me about Helen Holland?"

"First, because of doctor/patient privilege, there are limits on what I can discuss with you, Detective."

"Can you confirm for me that she was under your care?"

"Was under my care!" He emphasized the word, 'was.' He flipped closed the thick manila folder in front of him.

"When did your relationship with Helen Holland end?"

"When her husband removed her from Miami Medical Center."

"Why is she no longer under your care?"

"Mrs. Holland suffered from depression and displayed psychotic tendencies. Her husband, Thomas, insisted on taking her from the hospital. I objected and warned him of the consequences. He and I agreed; if he removed her from the hospital against my advice, I would no longer be responsible for her care."

"What were the consequences?"

"I advised Mr. Holland that Helen was dangerous in every respect. But he insisted that she would be better off at home."

"And what does 'dangerous in every respect' mean to you, doctor?"

"She was suicidal."

"Did you know that she was capable of murdering her family, Doctor?"

"Yes, I did, and I explained that specific danger to Mr. Holland. I told him she was a danger to herself and her family. I couldn't have made it any clearer."

"And what was his response?"

"He insisted on taking her home. He felt she would be better off surrounded by her family. I can only speculate that he didn't believe how sick his wife was."

"What was she suffering from, Doctor?"

"I can't go into the specifics, Detective, without the supervision of the court. I can assure you that this will become a civil matter and I need to be careful how I handle this. But, I can promise you, that Mrs. Holland was mentally ill in the extreme, capable of suicide and homicide. After clear warnings from me and the hospital, Mr. Holland chose to ignore those warnings and removed her from our care."

"During my interview with Mrs. Holland a few hours ago, I asked her if she thought what she'd done was wrong. She said that she knew what she'd done was wrong. That she'd planned this for a month or more. Does that sound like someone crazy to you?"

"Detective, I want to make one thing plain to you. Mrs. Holland isn't of sound mind. She's no more responsible for what happened this morning than you are. This tragedy was preventable. The crime was her husband insisted on her release from the hospital. None of this would have happened if he'd listened to me. That's the crime!"

"Can I get a copy of her file?"

"Not without a court order."

"Then will you turn over the material?"

"When we finish here, I'll turn the entire matter over to my attorney for handling. I just want you to know that it makes me angry that this has happened. There was no reason for it. That's the point I want to make."

"Do you have anything to corroborate your assertion that you released Mrs. Holland from the hospital against your advice?"

"I didn't release her. The hospital didn't release her. Her husband removed her from the facility. And, yes. I documented it in detail in the release papers her husband signed. My attorney will have copies of them."

"You knew this would happen, didn't you?"

"Not that it would happen, Detective, but that it could happen. Before you pass judgment, I did everything

I could. If I had had the legal power to prevent her husband from removing her from the hospital, I would have used it without hesitation. That's another discussion for another time. "

"There was nothing else you could do?"

"I'll share this much with you, and I hesitate to go that far. But it is important to me that someone understands the senselessness of what happened. Electroconvulsive Therapy is an effective treatment for those suffering from severe psychosis. Had Mr. Holland given me the freedom to use that mode of treatment, the outcome would have been much different. He refused to allow me to use it. Again, I can't tell you how angry this makes me."

Mario understood that anger.

Detective Willis Johnson was the only Negro detective at the Broward County Sheriff's office. Assigned the Holland case at eight this morning, he went to the Holland home after Mario Moretti had secured the scene. Moretti requested that he look over the crime scene with the Hollywood PD Identification Bureau. Satisfied that the Hollywood PD had done a thorough job, Johnson stopped by their offices and picked up a typed copy of Moretti's interview of Helen Holland. Then he returned to the Sheriff's office in Fort Lauderdale. Moretti had called to tell him that he'd transferred the suspect to the Broward County Jail. Moretti said he would meet him at the Sherriff's Office after he'd run down a lead.

Mario Moretti drove north to the Sheriff's headquarters near the Broward County Courthouse. Willis Johnson sat at one of two-dozen desks crammed into a space designed for twelve. Mario had worked with the tall, muscular man who'd retired from the Philadelphia PD and had been with the department as long as he'd been in Hollywood. He liked him. They had worked together on several cases.

When Mario walked into the squad room, 'Will' had his nose buried in a yellow legal pad and said to Johnson, "You gonna offer a guy a cup of coffee?"

"Sorry, we don't serve "I" talians here, Moretti," he said still looking down at his notes. "Hell, they won't even let me get a cup outta the white man's break room. Besides, one sip of that shit would stop a charging buffalo in its tracks."

Johnson finally looked up.

Moretti offered him a tall takeout coffee from a local donut shop. "Here, I didn't tell them what color you were."

"What, no donuts?"

"After what happened this morning, I won't eat for a month."

"It was bad enough seeing that scene after medics removed the bodies. I don't know if I could have handled that."

"You see her? The Holland woman?"

"Mario, I got bedbugs at home bigger than her. I'll bet she ain't eighty pounds with spray on her hair. After I read the transcript of your interview, I went over to the jail and talked with her myself. She repeated to me what she'd told you; that she was a bad mother, and that they couldn't go on living. She said she knew that it was wrong and she kept repeating to me that she was sane."

"You buy that? That she was sane?"

"I have no idea what sane is, man. We deal with all the sick bastards of this world, Mario. They're all crazy as far as I'm concerned. Who's to know who is and who isn't.

That takes someone a whole lot smarter than me to figure out. Hell, a lotta folks think I'm fruitier than a loon working this job, a lone raisin in a room full of snowflakes. I should have my own head examined."

"Let's get out of this fish bowl and get our stuff together before we go see Richter."

Moretti and Johnson found an empty conference room, and spread their files on the table. They sat on opposite sides of the table.

Johnson asked Mario, "Do you think she's faking it? Insanity, I mean?"

"When I see what that monster did to those children, I could give a rat's ass about whether she was sane or not. She should fry for what she did to those babies."

"That doesn't answer my question, Mario."

It was tempting, Mario thought, to squelch his interview with the shrink. Why, he reasoned, should he make it easy for her after what she did? "I went by her shrink's office and talked with him. He said that she'd been in a psychiatric ward and her husband insisted they let her out. The doc says he warned him that she could harm herself or others if he pulled her from the hospital; that she was psychotic and dangerous. The stupid bastard didn't listen to him."

"You're kidding!"

"Doc said flat out, that she was not to blame for what happened. That he could have prevented this, if her husband had listened to him."

"I've interviewed a lot of murder suspects. She was just creepy. Cold, you know? She talked about what happened like she was talking about having Sunday dinner with the family."

"She was that way this morning."

"You need to fill out a report on your conversation with the Doctor. Richter will need it." Johnson pushed back away from the table. "Did you see the throng of sharks circling outside?"

"The reporters? Yeah. I don't envy Richter. When the public finds out about this, they're going to look for someone to string up."

After he filled out a supplemental report on his conversation with Helen Holland's psychiatrist, Mario rode with Johnson to the State Attorney's office. Jonathon Richter, the assistant SA, occupied a twelve by twelve office. His furniture provided the foundation for several stacks of case files. Mario had never met Richter, although he had a reputation as a tough and ambitious prosecutor.

Richter was a baldheaded, robust man in his mid-forties.

Mario shook the firm hand of the man who would handle the case once they filed charges and the judge signed a warrant.

Each in turn, they conveyed what they had learned in their investigation.

"It's been on the news all morning. My phone has been ringing off the hook. I've heard of cases where mothers have killed their children, but nothing like this. Who handled the crime scene?"

Mario said, "Hollywood PD. Since this was such a heinous crime, I asked the Sheriff's Department to look in on the scene to corroborate that our people followed procedure and to offer help if needed. They assigned Will."

Richter said, "That was smart. If this goes to trial, especially a case like this, the defense will try to shred everything we did."

Mario said, "What do you mean, 'if this goes to trial?'"

"With the testimony of her shrink, even a wet-behind-the-ears defense attorney will demand a psych-eval. The chances of going to trial look pretty dim."

Johnson said, "Jon, I read the interview Mario did, and I interviewed her. She admits to the murders. She acknowledges she was sane at the time. She told both of us that she understands that what she did was wrong."

"Doesn't mean a thing. It all comes down to what the shrinks think."

Mario had to stuff down his anger. "If this was some guy who just blew away his family, we would go for the jugular. Because it's a woman. . ."

"Whoa, whoa. We're getting way ahead of ourselves. That call isn't mine to make. I'm with you; I think we should charge her with first-degree murder of every one in that family. From what you told me, she premeditated these homicides. We don't have a choice but to charge her. It is up to others to determine if she was sane when she did it. The county judge is liberal. I don't think he'll wait for defense motion for a psych-eval. He'll order it. And think about it for a minute. With that statement from her shrink, how could he not in good conscience consider it?"

"Someone needs to pay for what happened to those children, Mr. Richter."

"That's not our job, Detective Moretti. Our job is to find out who committed the crime, charge them, arrest them and present the evidence. A job I need to get back to doing. If you'll wait a few minutes, I'll have an affidavit and warrant prepared for you to take to Judge Mann for signature." Richter stood signaling the end of their discussion. "One more thing, Will. This woman is psychotic. We need to alert the jail to put her on suicide watch. That's the last thing we need right now."

"Already, done."

Mario waited for the documents, drove back to the Sheriff's office with Johnson and delivered the papers to Judge Mann's office at the Broward County Courthouse. The judge would issue a warrant, the court would follow procedures and the system would commit a travesty of justice.

He drove back to Hollywood. He wanted to make sure that the girl, Jody, was okay. He felt helpless that he couldn't do more. However, he could see to it that the girl was well cared for and that they protected her from the sensational elements of the case.

At the entrance to the hospital, reporters and television crews held a vigil under the watchful eyes of two uniformed police officers. At the nurse's station Mario stood waiting for clearance to see the girl.

The charge nurse said, "She kept asking for a friend of hers to come and see her. I think it is a boyfriend. She was so distraught, so we sent for him." She looked down at her notes. "Jackie McNamara. They were classmates. I gave them about twenty minutes together. He just left a few minutes ago. That calmed her down, but she's still tearful. Poor thing. So go easy, okay?"

"I don't need to question her, I just wanted to come and see her. Have any of her family come yet?"

"Her aunt is on her way from Atlanta. She should be here in a few hours or so."

"Are they going to let her go home with her?"

"Not sure. That will be up to her aunt. The psychologist assigned to her case thinks we should keep her here for a few days. According to her, she needs to talk about what happened and work through it. She thinks if she leaves the hospital without the proper care, she won't deal with it and it could cause problems in the future." Call buttons from several rooms buzzed on a console in front of her. "She's in room thirty-one. Ten minutes, okay? And again, go easy." She pointed down the hall to his right, silenced the buzzers and headed down a hall to his left.

Rodriguez was sitting with Jody Holland. Mario stood in the hall, caught Rodriguez's eye and motioned for her to come out of the room. "How's she doing?"

"She just sits there, on the bed, staring out the window, crying. I've tried to comfort her and engage her, but she's inconsolable. "

"Give us a minute."

Mario walked back into the room. Jody looked at him, bolted from the bed, threw her arms around his neck and hugged him. "I knew you would come." She latched on to him like a drowning man to a lifeguard.

"Okay, it's okay," he said, rocking her back and forth.

"It just doesn't seem real to me." She loosened her grip on his neck and pulled away.

Mario didn't know what to say to a child who had this level of physical and emotional trauma visited on her. "So you had a friend come to see you?"

Jody Holland backed into one of two chairs that sat on the window side of the bed. "Yes, Jack."

Mario pulled a few Kleenex from a box on the nightstand, handed them to her and sat opposite her. "Is he special to you?"

"Yes. My aunt will take me to Atlanta and I'll never see him again." She began to cry in earnest.

Jody sat on the edge of her chair with her head down.

Mario slipped out of his chair, knelt on one knee in front of her, lifted her chin with his right forefinger and said, "Does he feel the same way about you?"

"Yes."

"Then it will work out. You will see him again. It may not be right away. It may be several years, in fact. If what you say is true, then it will happen. Right now, you need to be with your family. What happened to you this morning is going to take some time to heal. You will have to be strong. Can you do that for me?"

She nodded. "Why did my mom do this?"

He said without conviction, "Your mom isn't well, Jody. She's sick. I don't know why she did it, and your mom doesn't know either. She was not in her right mind."

"Are they going to arrest her?"

"Yes. They already have."

"Will she try to hurt me again?"

"Sweetie, we locked her up in a place where she can't hurt you and she'll be there a long time."

"I wish I had died with the rest of them. I feel so alone."

"I know you feel bad, Jody. I wish I could change what happened. Your aunt will be here soon and she'll take good care of you."

The charge nurse came to the door and let Mario know that his time was up. "We've some tests to do, Detective."

Before Mario stood, he hugged the girl. "I'll be praying for you, Jody."

She hugged him. "I wish you could stay with me."

"Me too. But, your aunt will be here soon and things will get better, I promise."

As Mario backed out of the room, he regretted his words were so inadequate. He'd hoped to comfort her and failed. He kept thinking of his own daughter and wished there was more he could do. He couldn't, as was so often the case in his job. He dealt with the aftermath, beyond which help was often too late.

As he left the hospital and headed back to the station, he wondered how this would affect Jody long term. There was no way that a child that age would go through the carnage of the morning without some significant scars.

Six

Key West

1996

When I got up, Jody had opened the French doors to a small deck behind her clapboard house. She sat at a PVC pipe table and chair set, reading a newspaper. A sand-colored shade-cloth umbrella, in the center of the table, blocked the morning sun.

"I was beginning to think I would have to eat lunch alone," she said, not looking up from her paper.

I kissed her on top of her head and said, "I haven't slept that well in ages."

"Hmmmm," she cooed. "Wonder why?"

I took the seat opposite her and said, "Must have been that mattress." Jody had woven her hair into a single braid that dangled down the back of her neck past her shoulders. She wore no make-up and didn't need it. Except for telltale wrinkles at her eyes and the corners of her mouth, she looked thirty-eight not forty-eight. She wore a way-too-large, threadbare, Sloppy Joes tee shirt that hung off a tanned shoulder.

She looked at me and grinned. "Ah huh." Long pause so I didn't miss the tongue in cheek. "You want coffee? Just made it."

"Please." She got up, walked a few steps into the tiny, single-walled kitchen. She reappeared with a cup and a small tray with cream and artificial sweetener. "Did I remember that right?"

"Perfect." I mixed my concoction and took a sip. "How involved do you want to be in digging up the past? Yesterday it sounded like you wanted me to shield you from all but the essential details. Am I reading that right?"

"That's the way I felt until you got here yesterday. I think I would like to do it with you. I couldn't manage it alone. In fact, I wouldn't do it alone."

"I'm glad you want to be a part of it. I worried about deciding what information to keep from you. Of course, it would be marvelous to have you with me."

"You have any thoughts about where to start?"

"I thought we would begin with the newspaper accounts. I remember reading about it for weeks in the Hollywood Sun-Tattler and Miami Herald."

"They would have copies that far back?"

"I don't think they would have hard-copies. But the information should be on microfiche at the library. I remember going to the library when I was in high school to research old newspaper articles. They'll have records of all the newspapers there."

Jody said, "What about court records? I do remember, when I was sixteen, my mother's attorney sued my father's estate for a part of my father's life insurance settlement. I remember at the time it made me angry. My mother murders my father then expects to collect on his life insurance."

"What happened?"

"I have no idea. My aunt and uncle would never discuss anything with me. The only reason I know about it was that I overheard their conversation."

I said, "I remember all the secrets my mother kept from me as a child; the fact that I had a sister, Billie, for example. They think they're protecting you, but, in the end, it does a lot of damage."

"I don't think my aunt was protecting me. She just didn't want to deal with it. When she took me to Atlanta, we never spoke about my mother. She treated the whole situation as though it never happened. I wanted to talk about it, but couldn't. I had it bottled up and no place to vent it. I was so angry. I blamed myself. I felt like I could have stopped it. And I felt guilty that I survived."

Long silence, and then she said, "Jack, do you think I'm doing the right thing? This all seems so pointless."

"When I came to the Keys, looking for Billie, I was a mess, wasn't I?"

She leaned forward in her chair and rested her elbows on the table. "Yes, I felt so bad for you."

"And what did you encourage me to do?"

"Find the truth."

"What your mother did was horrible. There is more to this story than the tragedy itself. Whether you decide to meet with your mother or not, you need to find the truth, Jody.

"And the truth will set you free."

"Something like that. I still hate your mother for what she did to your family, what she did to you. Look how long I hated my mother for what she did to Billie only to find out my father was the guilty party."

"How soon do you want to start?"

"I hoped we could leave this afternoon, if we can get a room in Hollywood. This is spring-break in Fort Lauderdale and hotel rooms from Palm Beach to South Beach are booked."

She asked, "I wonder if the Sea Ray Motel is still there."

"You lived there while your father renovated your house."

"Yes, but I was living there when you and I met at the Casino Pool. I wonder if the pool is still there?

"The city pool's gone. The city bulldozed it in the seventies. The Sea Ray is now The Vagabond and it's still there. I stayed there last year. They remodeled it, but it's still the same place."

On the drive to Hollywood from Key West, Emily called.

"Hi, Jack, how are you?"

"Good, Em." I looked at Jody, who was not amused. "What's up?"

"I got a call from Nathan Barksdale."

Nathan Barksdale was the president of Reynolds and Ryan, my former publisher. "Why would he be calling you? He fired me remember? He no longer wanted an affiliation with me." I was still seething over the involuntary break with a company for whom I had written seventeen successful novels.

"Advanced sales of "The Tainted Lady," have far exceeded R&R's expectations, and reviewers are hailing it as your best work so far."

"So what does this have to do with Barksdale?"

"I called him a week ago."

"What?"

"Before you blow a fuse, hear me out. We've heard back from two publishing houses, who want to handle your work. And, I was wrong, Jack. Despite your public bout with depression, they're offering more money than R&R did in advances. After listening to Barksdale's 'no-one-in-the-industry-will-want-you' speech, I called him to thumb my nose at him. When I told him which publishers had stepped up, you could hear him salivate over the phone. He called me yesterday in a panic and wants to meet with you. I told him no. He called me this morning and said that he would beat any offer we had on the table."

"Why would that interest me? There is no way I would work with them again. I don't care how much money they offer me."

"I know that, Jack. I thought you might like the pleasure of telling him to buzz-off in-person. He said he would meet you in Key West. I would like to fly down and go over the other offers we have. If you want, I'll set up the Barksdale meeting. I've been working with Lisa and if Barksdale flies down, she wants in on the meeting, too."

"I'm not in Key West right now. I'm headed to Hollywood. Shouldn't be there more than a few days. Why don't you set it up for late next week, although I don't know what good it will do. Are you the one who pulled these publishers in or do I have Ms. Catera to thank?"

"Lisa and I have been working together, but it was her contacts and her charm. She's still earning her agent's fee, Jack. What's going on in Hollywood?"

"Research for a project I'm working on." I looked over at Jody and rolled my eyes.

"Alright. I'll call when the meeting is set up."

"Thanks, Em."

I closed the flip phone and laid it on the seat.

"I had been so focused on my own problems I had forgotten that they fired you, Jack. I feel awful now, dumping all my problems on you at such a stressful time."

"Jody, it isn't a problem. I'm glad it happened. I would like to try my hand at writing something different – a new direction. Genre fiction is restrictive and it is difficult after twenty-five plus novels to find something new to write. It's nice not to have a deadline. I want to enjoy this break."

"This isn't stressful to you?"

"No. We're together, with no restrictions on our time. What could be better?"

Hollywood Beach

We found a room at the Vagabond Motel on the north beach. It was the same ground floor room I stayed in last year, with a patio facing the ocean and a sliding glass door that opened onto the Broad Walk. The Broad Walk was a macadam strip the length of Hollywood Beach that separated the beach from the structures that lined it. It was open to foot and bicycle traffic only. The patio was cramped with two white vinyl web chairs and a small cocktail table between them. A knee-high hedge separated the patio from the Broad Walk, providing little privacy.

We checked into our room, opened the slider, stepped out onto the porch and took in a sight familiar to both of us. Running perpendicular to and between A1A and the Broad Walk, were many streets that dead-ended into the Broad Walk. At the end of each street, a park-bench faced the ocean and functioned as a barricade to vehicular traffic. When I first met Jody, her father had rented temporary quarters at the Vagabond. Our home was a few blocks south on another dead-end street near the Hollywood Beach Hotel. Jody's family had only been in their remodeled home less than a month before the tragedy.

Jody said, "What I remember most about this beach is you."

"Do you remember this motel?"

"Yes. We had several rooms, and Mom and Dad had a kitchenette. My grandparents came down from Pennsylvania to help Dad while Mom was in the hospital. They only stayed for a couple of weeks. They were here when I met you. Dad had just started a new job at Port Everglades."

"I remember when we met at the soda fountain on Johnson Street. Your grandmother had only let you leave for half-an-hour."

"Is my old house still there? I can't remember what it looked like."

"Yes." I wasn't going to suggest we go see it. It had to be something she wanted to do.

"Let's walk," she said.

I locked the sliding glass door and led her through a small break in the hedge onto the Broad Walk. "Where to?"

"I want to walk by where the old pool was and see Johnson Street."

"The drug store is now a tee shirt shop. You won't recognize it."

We walked south a few blocks to Johnson Street that teed into the Broad Walk. At the top of the tee, the city had erected a stage that faced down the center of Johnson Street. The city had closed the street to vehicular traffic to accommodate concerts.

Jody steered me onto the sand behind the stage.

"Let's sit for a minute."

We stooped down and sat Indian-style on the sand. The sun was low, casting long shadows from the coconut palms across the sand. The late afternoon air was balmy and the surf was calm, lapping at the sand. An old woman sat nearby casting breadcrumbs at seagulls that were frantic for something to eat.

Jody looped her arm through mine. "I remember this spot. This is where you kissed me for the first time." She gave my arm a squeeze. We sat in silence for a few moments and let the on-shore sea breeze carry us back to simpler times and first love. I swiveled toward her, and kissed her on the lips.

"Thank you for bringing me here, Jack. I wish we were here without having to revisit the horrors of that summer. But sitting here, in this spot with you, was worth the trip. After my aunt took me to Atlanta, I held tight the memories of this place, the pool, this stretch of beach and the hours we spent here. This spot, in my mind's eye, was my safe place. Over the years, when I couldn't handle the circumstances of my life, I mentally came here to escape. I remember you would hold me and comfort me like you're doing now."

I said, "When you left, I would come here just about every day and sit in this spot and wonder where you were and what you were doing. I felt connected to you here. At the same time, it was on this beach that we both got off track, where the seeds of the difficulties we would both face took root."

"I know, Jack. And I know that I have to face it."

We sat in silence for a long while, washed by the ocean breeze as the sun slipped away and the streetlights along the Broad Walk blinked on. There was much about Jody's life that I didn't know. She told me about her brushes with the law when she was in her late teens, but the details were sketchy. I wanted to know more, but I knew she would tell me in her own time.

"I want to walk by my old house."

"You sure?"

"Yes. That's where it all began."

We walked south on the Broad Walk to Pierce Street, turned right and found her old Key West style two story home midway between A1A and the beach. The house looked the same. In 1961, Jody's parents had filled the broad porch with white-wicker furniture and Boston ferns. Only two rusted bicycles and several days of folded newspapers occupied the porch now.

We faced the house from the street, huddled together. She asked me, "I wonder if the people who own this place have any idea of what happened here?"

"I have often wondered about that. The house sat empty for several years after. It was empty when I moved away. Is anything coming back to you?"

"No, but I do remember the house and when we first moved in, and how excited we all were. I remember you meeting my mom and how she went on about what a great writer you were."

"I remember that, too. She was so kind to me. Then she sent my short story to her magazine. That kick started my career."

"She liked you, Jack. She thought you had a lot of talent."

Jody looked up and down the street then at the house again. "Okay, I'm good." She turned and led me back to the Broad Walk.

"Where do we begin?"

"I want to start at the library, but I've been wondering whether the police department has anything in their files."

"That was more than 30 years ago."

"It's a good place to begin.

Seven

Hollywood Florida

1996

The police department resided in a three story, modern structure, off Hollywood Boulevard. The desk sergeant was a female officer in her late forties.

"What can I do for you?"

Jody stood next to me wearing snug fitting jeans, sandals and a wide neck white tee shirt. She'd pulled her hair straight back into a ponytail.

I asked, "In 1961, you arrested Helen Holland for a homicide. We were wondering if you still have anything on file."

"Holland?" She asked. She then tapped at the keyboard on her terminal. "1961? Doubt it. We usually don't hold files for more than ten years." She made a few more keystrokes. "Okay, I have it!" The illumination of the computer screen reflected in her gray eyes. "Amazing! The case is still open. And yes, I have the case as still active."

"Is there any way we can see it?"

"I'm sorry I can't do that. But, I can give you a copy of the file if you're willing to pay the cost of the copies."

"Of course," I looked at Jody and smiled.

"Have a seat." She pointed to chairs lined against the opposite wall, "I'll call the records department and find out how they want to handle it." The round woman with graying hair picked up the phone and we took our seats and waited.

The desk sergeant hung up the phone and said. "Records will pull the file and tell me how long it will take."

Jody said to me, "The case is still open. What does that mean?"

"We'll ask. It is odd though."

In a few moments, the desk sergeant came out through a waist high door. "They tell me it is a large file, but they aren't busy right now and can have everything ready in fifteen to twenty minutes if you're willing to wait."

We both nodded, and off she went, making calls and nodding to us when she got off the phone. We came to the desk and Jody asked, "You mentioned earlier that the case was still open. What does that mean?"

The sergeant brushed a spray of hair off her forehead. She said, "It means that either the case never went to trial, or that the county hasn't informed us of the disposition of the case. In either event, we still show the case as active."

"What would the county have to do with it?"

"This involves a homicide. After the initial investigation, we would have turned the case over to the State Attorney's office in Broward County. You might check with them, perhaps they'll have more current information."

Thirty minutes later, we walked out of the police department. The desk sergeant informed us that the files didn't contain crime scene photos per department policy. That all the information the city had on the case was in the file.

It neared lunch. We got in the car and drove to an Italian restaurant on Hollywood Boulevard. The host showed us to a table. We ordered and I laid the Hollywood PD file out on the table and scanned through the folder. There was an 'Offense Report' filled out by detective Mario Moretti listing the homicides of the five members of Jody's family. The form listed Jody as the person who reported the crime to the police. There were 'Supplemental Reports' covering the interrogation of Jody's mother, reports from the Broward County Medical Examiner and reports from the Identification Bureau with regard to precise details of the crime scene. There were reports from each of the patrol officers who were the first to respond to the scene. There was an arrest record showing Jody's mother transferred to the custody of the State Attorney.

I passed the documents to Jody one at a time as I inspected them.

"Mario Moretti. That's the detective who came to the hospital to check up on me. It says here that he interviewed my mom shortly after it happened. God, I don't know if I want to read this or not." Jody looked out the window at the front of the restaurant then looked at me. Signs of stress showed on her forehead and the corners of her eyes. "I guess I wasn't expecting to get this much information so quick."

"Take your time. You don't need to go any faster than you want."

"Moretti. I wonder if he's still around."

I flagged down our server and asked if they had a phonebook. He returned with a three-inch thick book that contained listings for Miami, Hollywood and Fort Lauderdale.

I opened it and flipped through the Ms. "Moretti . . . Moretti . . . Mario Moretti. Got it. He's in the phonebook. Do you want me to call him?"

"Other than you, he's the only thing I remember about that day and how kind he was to me. I know it's a long shot, but let's try to call him."

I dialed the number reached a woman and asked, "I'm looking for Mario Moretti. He used to be a detective with the Hollywood Police Department. Do I have the right number?"

The woman excused herself and then a male voice. "Hello."

"My name is Jack McNamara."

"I know that name," Mario said with a gravelly voice.

"I'm calling about the Helen Holland case, from 1961."

Long silence. "I remember it and now I remember you. A writer, aren't you? Hollywood boy."

"One and the same."

"How can I help you, pal?"

"Jody Holland . . . "

"The girl who survived? I know that case like it was yesterday."

"Right. She's trying to reconstruct her memories of that time. She's here with me. Since you handled the case we wondered if you would agree to meet with us."

"Been off the job for more than twelve years. But I remember that little girl. I'll never forget her. I've wondered all these years about what happened to her. Meet with you?

Sure. If it will help that girl, I would be happy to help. Where are you now?"

"A little Italian restaurant on the main drag." I gave him the name.

"Know it well. Would now be alright? I'm busy this afternoon."

I put my hand over my cellphone and whispered that he would be willing to come now.

She nodded.

I said, "Now would be perfect."

"I'll be there in ten." I flipped the phone closed.

"He's on his way."

Jody focused on one of the reports in the file. "This is Moretti's interview with my mom an hour after it happened." She scanned the report. "She admits to shooting us all, my dad, all the kids. She shot us in birth order, oldest to the youngest."

"Does it say why?"

"All she says is that they couldn't go on the way they were going. That she was a bad mother. She kept repeating that they couldn't go on. She says she shot everyone in the head so they wouldn't suffer. That she was dead inside and that she had no emotions." She flipped a page and said, "It says that I prevented mom from using the gun on herself. That my wound was only superficial."

I scanned the autopsy reports. "All the gunshot wounds were to the head. Looks like your father heard the commotion and came to investigate and your mom shot him in the living room."

Jody began to tear up. "It was all so senseless."

Our server came and we ordered wine and waited for Moretti. The door chimed, and we both looked up as Moretti came through the door. Jody recognized the short stocky man immediately. She stood and met him with a ferocious hug.

Mario broke from the embrace. "Look at you. Not the little frightened girl I remember. And so beautiful."

Jody offered Moretti a seat. He had a thick manila envelope with him that he laid on the table in front of an empty chair. He took a seat.

Moretti spoke first. "In all my years on the job, there was no case that grabbed me that way. I'll never forget it. Horrible. Just horrible."

"You were so kind to me, Detective. I was so scared."

"I did what I could. But I never felt that it was enough. I gotta ask. It's been almost thirty-five years. Why are you digging into this now?"

"My mom wants to reconnect. She sent me a letter recently and wants to share her side of the story. I know so little. I thought before I agreed to meet with her that I should have all the facts."

Moretti had thick black wavy hair flecked with gray. He had a neat thick coal black mustache, a heavy beard and bushy eyebrows. He leaned in toward both of us and folded his fleshy hands on top of the table. "I would be happy to tell you what I know. But, I want you to know, up front, that I'm angry that she got off Scot-free. She should have paid for what she did to you and your family. If that's a problem for you, then perhaps you should . . ."

Jody said, "NO! No. I'm fine with that. I'm angry too. But what do you mean she got off free?"

"They released her in 1970 and the state dropped all the charges against her. I wrote letters, drove to Ft. Lauderdale to meet with the Assistant State Attorney, but it did no good. They let her go."

"Why?" I asked.

"They said that she was mentally incompetent when she committed the murders."

Jody said, "I was just reading through your interview with my mom and you asked her twice whether she knew that what she'd done was wrong. She even said . . . wait a minute," Jody flipped through the file, ". . . that she was sane and knew that what she did was morally and legally wrong."

"Two years after that happened, your mother's attorney, filed a suit in court claiming a share of your father's life insurance policy. They argued that your mother was mentally incompetent at the time of the murders. That entitled her to equal standing with you as an heir."

"I remember that," Jody said.

"The court ruled in your mother's favor because three psychiatrists ruled she was mentally incompetent to stand trial when she was arrested. Then, in 1970, when your mother was ready for release, her attorneys argued that the state should drop the arrest warrant. They reasoned since the court in 1963 had ruled that she was incompetent, the likelihood of a conviction if tried again was small."

A server came to get a drink order from Moretti.

"Just water," Moretti said.

"Have a glass of wine detective," Jody reached across the table and touched his forearm.

"Gave the stuff up years ago. I'm a much nicer person when I don't drink."

I asked, "What do you remember from the morning this all happened?"

"It is more like, what will I never forget about that morning. The pictures that I have in my mind no man should have to keep. It was those little babies with gunshot wounds to their temples. Them lying in their own blood. You, bleeding from your own wound, scared to death and traumatized. You were a brave little girl that morning. You took the gun away from your mother and had the presence of mind to call the police."

"I don't remember any of it," Jody said.

"It doesn't surprise me. No child should ever have to experience what you did that morning. When we got your mother to the station, she was as cold as ice. She talked about the murders as someone might talk about cleaning their house or washing their car. She chain-smoked. She looked you right in the eye with no remorse whatsoever. It was as if the devil herself sat across from me. At the house, when I first got there, the officers on the scene told me that she was desperate to get to the gun to take her own life."

Jody asked, "Why? Did she ever give you a good answer?"

"Nothing more than you have in that file. I've investigated homicides for more than thirty-five years. In my opinion, anyone who, with premeditation, takes the life of another has a mental defect. They're all crazy. If a man had done this, he would have fried in the electric chair. She took the innocent lives of four children that morning. They never got the chance to experience life or have families. Regardless of the reason, crazy or not, she should have rotted in a prison cell for the rest of her life. She should have at least stood trial. Where's she now . . . no, I don't want to know that."

"It is obvious that my mom's case has affected you. I'm so sorry, Detective. It is amazing how many people have suffered and lives altered from one person's actions."

Mario picked up the manila folder he'd placed on the table. "This is every shred of paper on your mother's case, everything in the public record. There are also copies of all the newspaper clippings related to the case. Now that you're here and I know you're okay . . ." he handed the envelope to Jody, "there is nothing more I can do."

"I remember you coming to the hospital to see me," Jody said. "Jack had just left and I was crying. Do you remember what you said to me?"

"That if he liked you, you would see him again."

Jody reached over and squeezed my arm. "You were right. It took a while, but he came back to me. It was the only shred of hope I had when I left for Atlanta. You gave me that hope when there was none. I'll never forget you, Detective."

"Mario."

"Mario," she said.

We drove back to the Vagabond and spread the contents of Moretti's file out on the king size bed. We passed documents back and forth. We followed the events from Helen Holland's arrest through her release from the South Florida Hospital in 1970.

The events from the day of the murders, in 1961, to the civil case, in 1963, were just as Moretti had described. The only correspondence between 1963 and 1969 were periodic letters related to the status of the patient. There were periodic reminders from the state that the hospital should return Holland to the jurisdiction of the court to face charges pending against her when she was ready for release.

Then in 1969, the hospital notified the Assistant State Attorney that Helen Holland had recovered. As Moretti had said, Helen Holland's attorney lobbied for her release using the incompetency ruling of the 1963 civil trial as justification. He argued that bringing the matter to trial would be a waste of the state's resources since the likelihood of a conviction was small. The court required testimony from three of the hospital's clinicians that she was neither a threat to herself or to others. With that provided, the court ordered her released and set aside the arrest warrant.

It was dinnertime before we absorbed all the information the files contained.

We knew in brutal detail, what happened. Would that satisfy Jody's need to know? I empathized with Moretti. The brutality of what happened demanded justice. This was senseless carnage, perpetrated on the sinless and defenseless. Someone needed to pay for what happened.

I put the last piece of paper down on the bed near Jody. She sat Indian-style on the bed, scooped up all the paper, straightened them into a neat pile and inserted them back into Moretti's envelope. Jody was a woman who always looked "together." She generally wore her hair in a ponytail and seldom was a hair out of place. She wore a small watch with a brown leather buckled band, a thin silver necklace with a single pearl and no other jewelry. While Emily always looked like a fashion model, Jody dressed in casual, simple, comfortable clothes. As I watched her set the file aside, her face wore the stress of the truth she'd uncovered. She looked at me, her brow lined and tight. Then the events of the day collided with her emotions. She reached up for me. I joined her on the bed and held her. We said nothing. There was nothing to say. She emptied herself, pulled back away, wiped her eyes on the sleeve of my shirt.

"I wanted to know, right?" she said, still sniffling.

"Knowing is one thing. What are you thinking?"

"It's too much to take in. I need a break, and a shower."

Eight

We returned to Vincent's Italian Restaurant for dinner. Servers had covered the bare tables at lunch with white cloth and lighted tea-candles. Jody wore an oyster-shell colored, ankle length, sleeveless dress that scooped at the neck and hugged her body. Her hair hung straight to just below her shoulders and her face had a hint of makeup.

We ordered wine, toasted the evening and sipped chilled Pinot Grigio. She looked more rested, her face cleansed of the stress I observed earlier.

"I love this little place. It's so charming," she said as she scanned the room that resembled a wine cellar in a Tuscan villa. "And even though the wine isn't expensive, it tastes scrumptious. Must be your company."

"I love that dress."

"I think you liked it better when I wasn't in it." The first smile of the day.

"You have me there. You're beautiful either way."

She said, "You make me feel special, Jack."

"I hope so, Jody, because you are special."

"What are your thoughts after you read all those files?"

"I understand what happened, but I'm not sure I understand why it happened."

"If I focus too much on it, I don't think I can do this, Jack. You're right though, I think understanding why is where I want to spend our energy. How could something like this happen? How could a mother kill her children? Her babies? Why would she want to kill me? We didn't do anything to her."

"Did you see the statement from her psychiatrist?"

"You mean my dad's insistence that she come home from the hospital and the doctor's warning that she was still suicidal and might hurt others? Yeah. That made it sound like my dad could have prevented this. I wasn't expecting that," she said.

"That set me back a little as well. If she was sick, then your father should have left her in the hospital."

"I do remember how much pressure he was under. Even with my grandparents staying with us, our stay at the motel was total chaos. I missed a lot of school and Dad missed a lot of work. He needed Mom to be there just to survive."

"Five kids can be a handful."

"You have no idea. Where do we go from here, Jack?"

"We're missing big chunks of information. From the time they arrested her, to the time they released her from the mental facility was roughly a nine-year blank page. What was wrong with her? We should try to find out. What happened to her after she got out of the hospital? That's another chunk of time we know nothing about."

"What did you think about Moretti's comment that the court should have punished her for what happened?"

"I have to be honest, Jody. When Moretti told us that she'd gotten off without a trial, I was angry. Then I read the detective's notes from her psychiatrist about how unstable she was; that your father had ignored the warnings about her mental state. I want to know more about your mother. Something isn't adding up."

"How do we find out?"

"Go to the hospital where she received treatment."

"Do you think they'll talk to us about her?"

"One way to find out. We could go there in the morning. All they can say is no."

"Okay. Let's try."

We ordered dinner, had some more wine and managed to slide the topic of Jody's mother aside for the evening. We were enjoying after-dinner-coffee when she asked me again about Emily.

"So Emily is coming to Key West?"

"I guess." I put as much exasperation in my voice as I could muster. I didn't want to talk about this.

"Does she know about me, Jack?" She fiddled with her necklace, sliding the single pearl back and forth on the silver chain.

"No. I had no reason to tell her."

"Are you hiding me?"

"When I came back from Key West after we reconnected, she was hell-bent on a divorce. I had done everything I could to make a go of it. If I told her about you, it would have been one more thorn on the pile of thorns. In the end, it wouldn't have mattered."

I was a little concerned she was bringing Emily up again so soon.

"What is she like?"

"You'll like her. In fact, if I had to guess, you two could be good friends."

"Is she pretty?"

"Yes," I said, feeling uncomfortable with where the conversation was going.

"Is she prettier than me?"

I didn't answer right away. I just looked into her eyes. "You're both beautiful, Jody. You have nothing to worry about. She has no interest in me."

"That's not what I'm worried about." She dropped the pearl and it fell down between her breasts. "You still love her."

"Jody."

"I know. I know. But I lost you once. And I don't want that to happen again."

"Let's not do this, okay. I'm here with you because I want to be here. My feelings are raw from the rejection and divorce. Time will take care of it. I'm enjoying my time with you."

She gazed at me. I could tell that she wanted to continue to talk about it and bit her tongue. I wished that Emily were not coming to Key West. It was too late to head her off. If Em were to continue to work with me and I had a relationship with Jody, Jody would just have to work through the issue.

Nine

South Florida State Hospital

The next morning we presented ourselves to the receptionist at the hospital lobby.

"Hi, my name is Jack McNamara. I wonder if it would be possible to talk with someone in administration?"

The Hispanic woman punched a few keys on the phone, spoke in low tones and said, "Someone will be with you in a moment."

Decorated in complementary shades of marine blue, the lobby was empty. We took seats closest to the receptionist. A lit aquarium bubbled across from us. Jody fidgeted with her small handbag and I rested my hand on her thigh to calm her.

A young woman in her late twenties dressed in scrubs approached. Dark hair, dark features and rail thin, she looked almost anorexic. "Hello, my name is Felicia," she extended a hand to Jody. Jody stood and shook it.

"Jody Holland."

I stood, extended a hand to her.

"What can I do to help you?"

Jody and I both began talking at the same time. I relented. Jody said, "In 1961, my mother was admitted to the hospital and released in 1970. I'm trying to find out as much information as I can about her stay."

"Alright. If you will follow me, I'll try to help."

Felicia led us down a hallway to a nondescript door. Inside, she showed us to seats in front of her desk in a small office.

Felicia asked, "And what was your mother's name?"

"Holland. Helen."

"Yes, I show that she was a patient." She tapped the keyboard in front of her terminal. "Yes, she was a patient during the years you mentioned. How can I help?" she said in a professional and distant tone.

"I was wondering if it were possible to obtain a copy of her file."

"Her patient files?"

"Yes."

"I'm afraid that information is confidential. I'm not even sure we still have those files since it has been more than twenty years since her discharge."

"Are any of her doctors that treated her still on staff?"

She tapped away at the keyboard. "Generally, our psychiatric patients are treated by a team of clinicians, not just one doctor." A few more keystrokes. "There is still one of the doctors who worked with your mother on staff. The rest have long since retired or left the hospital."

I asked, "Is there any way we could meet with him?"

"Her." More keystrokes. "Dr. Carnes heads the psychiatric department. If you will wait here, let me find out if she's in the hospital this morning."

Felicia left us sitting in front of her desk and disappeared back into the hall. I looked at Jody. "So far so good."

Five minutes later, Felicia returned with passes she asked us to pin to our clothes. "She's in, and will spend a few moments with you."

We rode an elevator to the second floor then walked to a suite of offices, entitled "Clinical Services." Felicia shepherded us past the clerk to an open office. The badge on the door read, "Dr. Janis Carnes."

Carnes was a large woman in her early to mid-sixties, with tight curled natural gray hair and dressed in an ill-fitting suit. Her face was fleshy, pale and pleasant. Spider plants hung from macramé hangers and a stained glass panel hung in her window diffusing the bright sunlight.

Felicia made introductions and departed. We all shook hands and we sat in two guest chairs in front of her desk.

Carnes spoke first. "You're inquiring about Helen Holland?"

Jody answered, "Yes, I'm her daughter."

"And you sir?"

"I'm just a friend of Jody's – here for moral support."

"What information are you hoping to find, Ms. Holland?"

"Please call me, Jody. Before I answer your question, can I assume that you were one of my mother's doctors?"

"Yes. I joined the staff in 1964; she'd already been a patient here for three years. But I was involved in her treatment and care until we released her."

"Then you know what she did?"

"If you're referring to the homicides, yes, I'm familiar. You were the only surviving child."

"I want to know why. How could such a senseless thing happen?"

"Normally, I wouldn't be able to discuss her case with you because of doctor-patient confidentiality. But I encouraged your mother to reach out to you when she was first released and I have continued to do so over the years. She'd hoped that one day you would come looking for her and I have her permission to answer any questions you may have." Carnes pushed back in her chair. "I was beginning to wonder whether that day would ever come. And I'm getting close to retirement. So I'm glad you came."

"What was wrong with her?"

"Do you want a short answer?"

"I want to understand. Whatever that takes."

"Alright. In 1961 when all this happened to your mother, we didn't know a lot about Postpartum Mood Disorders. Today, there is still much we don't understand. Many women following the delivery of a baby suffer from what we call the baby blues. This mild depression presents a few days to a week following delivery. It can last a few days or a few weeks. This is normal. The female body experiences dramatic swings in hormone levels as it adjusts following childbirth. Again, these episodes are transitory. A small percentage of women experience severe depression. And even more rare are women who have psychotic episodes.

"What we didn't know then is that the psychosis can occur differently in different women depending on their mental health history. For example, a woman suffering from bi-polar disorder who becomes pregnant is fifty-percent more likely to contract Postpartum Psychosis, PPP for short. Women who suffer from schizophrenia are also fifty-percent more likely to suffer from PPP. And the treatments for each of these disorders are different. PPP also strikes mothers who've had no previous mental illness. In your mother's case, she had no prior history of mental illness before the birth of her last child. Her four previous pregnancies were normal. This is why there was no advanced warning of her condition. So to answer your specific question, your mother suffered from rapid onset of psychosis as a result of her last pregnancy.

"I know you have more questions." She held up a finger. "Let me just tell you this and then you can fire away. Last year there were roughly 3.8 million births in the U.S. If the statistics hold true, 3,800 mothers will have experienced PPP. Of those mothers, roughly 300 will have committed suicide, infanticide or both. It is rarer still for a mother to take the life of her entire family. In the latter case, there are no statistics to draw from. But, let me assure you that cases like your mother's come along once in two or three decades."

Jody asked, "And you have no idea what caused it?"

"Because these cases are so rare, there isn't a lot of research; only speculation. There is a school of thought that the trauma of childbirth causes PPP. This was the case with your mother's last childbirth. She experienced a difficult, painful delivery. Think of it as post-traumatic stress at a time when a mother's hormones are off the charts. Childbirth pushes a mother's mind and body to the limit. The cocktail of chemicals the body produces skews the brain in ways we're still trying to understand. To produce the level of psychosis your mother experienced, the body created a perfect chemical storm in her brain. I'm convinced that the trauma of childbirth was the cause of your mother's PPP."

"She was in the hospital, why didn't they recognize the problem?"

"I have asked that same question. The answer will disappoint. I went back through her medical records, and there were diagnostic errors right from the beginning. For example, doctors need to treat PPP immediately. The longer they delay treatment the more deep-rooted the problem can become. Had her doctors diagnosed her properly, when they first admitted her to the hospital, she could have been back to a normal state in a matter of weeks. Unfortunately, her obstetrics doctor diagnosed her as having the 'baby blues' and prescribed bed-rest. So, they put her in the hospital without treating her underlying condition, nor did they recognize the symptoms of a worsening psychosis. So they released her from the hospital and her psychosis worsened."

Jody said, "I remember that, when she came home from the hospital the first time, she locked herself in her room and didn't want to have anything to do with the baby. My dad said that she just needed rest and to leave her alone."

"And that was devastating for your mother. She needed immediate help and didn't get it. After a month went by and she worsened, your father took her back to her psychiatrist. That was a good move. They put her into a mental facility. Unfortunately, when doctors recommended ECT to combat the psychosis your father wouldn't approve it. He tied the doctor's hands. With this restriction, they treated her for a garden-variety clinical depression, when they should have taken aggressive action.

"What made it worse was your father's impatience with her progress and his belief that your mother needed to be home around people who loved her and could care for her. In time, the hospital might have convinced your father to allow ECT. But your father removed your mother from the hospital, and that option was no longer on the table."

Jody asked, "What is ECT?"

"In the early sixties, we didn't have the psychotropic drugs we have today. Thorazine was the only drug available to help with severe psychosis. The main weapon available at the time and this modality is still in use today, is Electroconvulsive Therapy or ECT."

I asked, "Is this the electroshock therapy they used on Hemingway?"

Carnes got up, wheeled her rolling chair around to our side of the desk and sat down. "Yes. Again, we don't know exactly why, but ECT treatments have a way of resetting the brain and they can ease the symptoms of psychosis. The convulsive reaction the body has to ECT creates this reset. There are several ways to produce convulsions, but electrostimulation of the brain is the safest. Think of rebooting your computer when glitches invade the operating software. Had we used ECT early on, Jody, I'm convinced that none of this would have happened to your mother. Her psychosis would have been short-lived."

"You make this sound like PPP, or whatever you call it, is a temporary condition." Jody turned her chair to square up to Carnes.

"It is temporary! Most women who suffer from PPP, who have proper treatment are back to normal in months. For your mother, who didn't receive the right type of treatment soon enough, her recovery was longer."

"How much longer?"

"I would say that she was physically healthy within two-and-a-half years. Emotionally it was a different story.

The physical and chemical imbalances that caused your mother's psychosis subsided with treatment. If there hadn't been the taking of life, we could have released her from the hospital in six months and handled the rest of her recovery as an outpatient. The taking of life, caused by her mental condition, created issues on another level that took several years to treat. Even though your mother was physically well, the emotional damage done by the lives she took created an enormous challenge in treatment. Before we talk about the treatment any further, I want to make a point. Your mother isn't responsible for what happened!"

I blurted out, "How can you say that after what she did? She took the lives of four innocent children and in such a brutal fashion."

"I can assure you, Mr. McNamara, that Mrs. Holland had no idea what she was doing. Her reality was so disrupted she believed that taking the lives of her children was the only choice she had. I know that it is difficult to comprehend, Jody, but your mother's mind was so scrambled she didn't know what was real and what was not."

Jody said, "In the police interrogation that I read last night, she told Detective Moretti she had no emotion–she was dead inside."

"The horror of the place your mother was in, in her mind, was so real that she felt she needed to protect her family from it. The only way she knew to do that was to take her own life and take her family with her. In her state of mind, she believed that she had to save her family from sliding into Hell. She loved you. She wanted to save you."

"Jesus," Jody said. "You're certain that she believed that?"

"Yes. I have hours of taped interviews the doctors recorded following her admission to the hospital. She believed that she had no choice. That her family would fall into Hell because of her and that she had to do something. I have the authority to release those tapes to you if that would convince you of what I'm saying."

"I believe you, Doctor. Did she admit to killing her family?"

"In the beginning, yes. Then after ECT treatments, she began to deny that any of it happened. She put up a wall to protect herself from the horrible truth of what she'd done. Treating her PPP was straightforward. Helping her to face the reality of her actions, and then to live with the consequences: now that took some time."

"If what you say is true, then it must have been horrible for her."

"Yes. It was and it still is. There is no way to escape the horrors of that morning in 1961, even though she was out of her mind. The person who committed those heinous crimes all those years ago was not your mother. That's the tragedy of her story. She was not responsible. This was not her fault, but, she has to live as though it were."

I said, "But where's the justice in all this? She took five innocent lives."

"May I call you, Jack?"

"Of course."

"I'm sensing that you have strong feelings for Jody. Everything in your body language tells me that. Am I right?"

I looked at Jody, smiled and said, "Yes."

"What if I were to hypnotize you, convincing you that someone was about to torture Jody in a most brutal way.

Suppose I convinced you, under hypnosis, that if you shot her, you would spare her from the worst torture imaginable. What if you were so convinced of the truth of that reality, you took a gun and took her life so that she wouldn't suffer. Suppose that after you had taken Jody's life, I brought you out of your hypnotic state and I presented you with Jody's dead body. How do you think you would feel? You would deny it, until I showed you pictures of you pulling the trigger. How would you feel then?"

I didn't say anything.

"That's what happened to Helen Holland. So convinced was she of the horrors that awaited her family, she took their lives to spare them. Make no mistake, Jack. She has paid. She's paying and will continue to pay for the crimes she committed. This is a horrendous penalty for an act that, by every measure, was not her fault."

Jody asked, "So how did you treat her?"

"Once her psychosis abated, her treatment consisted of one-on-one talk therapy and group therapy. Progress was slow at first, until another PPP patient, who'd taken the life of her baby, came into our facility. Your mother took her under her wing and poured herself into helping her. Only then did she begin to heal."

Jody asked, "When was the last time you talked to her?"

"Three months ago. She called me when she decided to try to contact you."

"You think I should meet with her." A statement not a question.

"I can't make that call for you, but I think you would both benefit from reconnecting."

"I don't know," Jody said with pessimism. "It seems so overwhelming."

"Have you been through counseling? That was an awful thing to happen to a fourteen year old girl."

"Yes. It was many years after, but yes. I'm still so angry about it. I don't know that I could forgive her for what she did."

"Well, here is what I would like you to do. I've put a file together that contains information that will support what I told you today. I want you to take it with you and I want you to review it in detail. Included are magazine and news clippings that tell the story of your mother and her work since she left the hospital all those years ago. She's a remarkable woman, Jody. I hope, as you know more, you will change your mind about her. As a doctor, I can tell you the events in 1961 haunt your mother as much they haunt you. Forgiveness is an amazing medication and treatment."

"I should have a lot more questions, but I don't."

"It is a lot to digest." Doctor Carnes stood, and Jody and I stood with her. She pushed her chair back behind her desk, took a business card out of the pencil drawer and scribbled on the back of the card. "Here is my personal number. If you think of something, call me anytime. Your mother is an amazing woman. I'll say some prayers that the two of you get reacquainted."

She escorted us to the elevator and we said our goodbyes.

Dr. Carnes hugged Jody and said, "I hope I helped."

"You did. Thank you. At least I know the truth.

Ten

Hollywood

1996

We had a late breakfast at Denny's in West Hollywood and drove back to the motel. We changed into our bathing suits. We staked out a patch of sand near the water's edge, spread out a blanket we borrowed from the motel room and opened the file that Dr. Carnes had given us. As we'd done the previous day, with the Hollywood PD file, we passed papers back and forth until we'd both seen and read everything in Carnes' file.

It was 1965 before Helen acknowledged to doctors what she'd done. The treatment notes indicated that ECT therapy lasted for about three months and concluded in late 1961. From 1961 to 1965, she remained in a torpid shell, unresponsive but no longer a danger to herself. All the doctors involved in her treatment were male until the hospital assigned Carnes to her team and gave her the lead in the case. The hospital felt that Helen might respond to a female doctor.

From 1968 until her discharge from South Florida State Hospital, Helen Holland took supplemental college courses to meet the requirements for admission to medical school at the University of Florida, Gainesville. Dr. Carnes lobbied the head of the university's medical school for Helen's acceptance. Jody's mother passed the admissions exam and began school in the summer of 1971.

In the fall of 1975, Helen graduated at the top of her class. She did her doctoral thesis on postpartum disorders and began residency at Shands Hospital, Psychiatric Unit, in Gainesville, Florida. She remained in residence until 1980.

In the late 1970s, while still in residence, Helen founded a non-profit organization called, "You're Not Alone." She hoped to meet the needs of women suffering from Postpartum Disorders. She discovered, through her own experience, how little education law enforcement, the legal system, even the medical profession, including psychiatrists, had with regard to this disease. By the time she'd completed her residency requirements, she'd raised several million dollars by finding and networking with other women who'd suffered psychotic episodes following childbirth.

Dr. Carnes hired the fifty-eight year old Helen Holland in the fall of 1981, but Helen remained on staff for only two years. She'd convinced a private hospital in Tampa to join with her to create a treatment and research facility for women with reproductive mental disorders. The hospital devoted half a floor to patients and hired a small team to assist Helen in her research.

With several millions from the "You're Not Alone," organization, in partnership with the hospital, she formed, "Bay Area Postpartum Women's Health."

After more than a year of building staff, training, developing protocols and educating other mental health organizations in the southeast about their work, the treatment center opened in the spring of 1985, the day of Helen's 62th birthday.

Helen's pioneer work made her a natural as an expert witness in infanticide cases. Her experiences with ignorance in the legal system about PPP prompted her to form an alliance with a law firm in Tampa who specialized in representing these afflicted women. Antiquated laws throughout the US and differences in state laws present challenges in consistent fair treatment for PPP victims from state to state. She devoted hours lobbying state legislatures to change existing laws with mixed results.

In 1990, following five years of research into women's postpartum mental health issues, the research center published its findings. They had discovered and identified six different, distinct disorders following childbirth. Her team argued that each of the separate disorders required unique treatment. They discovered that treating a woman with undiagnosed bi-polar disorder with medications used for common postpartum depression, could push the patient into a manic phase, making the condition worse.

The contents of Dr. Carnes' file heralded a distinguished, selfless and unwavering humanitarian career.

Jody sat up on the blanket. We'd both finished reading about the same time.

"Jack, this is astonishing." Jody swept papers from the file into a small block and placed them back into the folder.

"Does it change the way you think about her?"

"I liked it better when she was a monster."

"Sounds like she's trying to atone for what she did."

"She could have become the Pope and I don't think I could forgive her for what she did, Jack."

"She lives in Tampa," I said.

"Yeah, I got that. And she's a shrink, no less. How ironic."

"Why didn't Carnes tell us about this?"

"Why didn't Mom just send us all this information in the mail? Why lead us on this magical mystery tour?"

I said, "You think she could be that clever? I don't think she could have known you would come looking for her. And the note she sent didn't suggest you do that."

Jody rubbed the outside of the file with her hand. "Knowing all this doesn't change anything. You can't believe how much I've suffered from what happened. From the events in her life, she took a lemon and made lemonade. When they should have punished her, they rewarded her. She took the horror of what happened and profited from it."

"You don't think she was trying to make up for what she did?"

"What value do you put on a human life? When you put the weight of the five lives she took on a scale, I don't think there is anything she could put on the other side to balance it out. She could do nothing in my mind to warrant forgiveness. Nothing!"

I wanted to argue with her. It was obvious that Jody's mother worked hard to pay for what she'd done. I thought about John Walsh, the television personality who hosted the show, "America's Most Wanted." In 1981, someone abducted Adam, his six-year-old son, from the Hollywood Mall and murdered him. John Walsh put his grief to work helping other families of abducted or mistreated children.

Walsh founded the Adam Walsh Child Resource Center, a non-profit organization dedicated to legislative reform. The organization merged with The National Center for Missing and Exploited Children (NCMEC).

He lobbied government and large corporations for changes in laws to beef up security at malls and retail stores. He helped create new procedures that would aid in the rapid location of abducted children. The most recognizable outcome of his work was the Amber Alert system.

Walsh's high public profile made him a celebrity and the unintended consequences were notoriety and wealth. Some might argue that he capitalized on the tragedy of his son's death for his own personal gain. I never saw it that way. Because of his unique experience, he was able to stand up for the victims of unspeakable crimes and speak for them. The fact that he profited from that position was a consequence not a goal.

John Walsh was not the perpetrator of the crime. He was as much the victim as Adam. That was where the analogy between Walsh and Helen Holland diverged. But both of these people encountered horrendous events and they healed through helping others. They worked to make sure that others didn't repeat the mistakes that contributed to their tragedy.

From everything I had learned, Helen Holland was a mentally disturbed woman who needed help and didn't get it. If I had to find blame, I would fault Jody's father for creating the environment for disaster. If anything, I empathized with Helen and the pain that she must live with.

I wanted to share all this with Jody, but I knew she was not in a place to hear it.

"What did you think of the correspondence between the hospital and the prosecutor's office on whether she should stand trial?" I thought it was better to ask questions at this point than to opine.

"You don't think she was guilty of anything do you? I can tell from your reaction." Her eyes narrowed.

I sat up on the blanket and tried to think of the right thing to say. "Jody, it isn't important what I think. I cannot begin to fathom the depths of your feelings on this. But, you have every right to be upset and angry. Whatever you decide to do, whether you agree to meet with your mother or not, I'm with you. Only you can decide what is right for you."

"But, I'm sensing you've changed your mind about her."

"I don't think my opinion would be helpful right now. We came here to gather information to seek the truth about what happened. I don't think it's the right time to draw conclusions. This is a lot of information to process, Jody." I put my hand on her bare knee and gave it a squeeze.

"Jack, I wanted you to come with me, because I trust your judgment. I would like to know what you're thinking."

"Okay. When we were talking with Carnes, she used the example of her putting me into a hypnotic state, and she gave me the choice between a mercy killing and someone torturing you; it got my attention. What it made me think of is my own serious bouts with depression. When I was at my low point, shortly before we reconnected, I would have taken my own life because I believed at the time that my life wasn't worth spare pocket change. I was no good to anyone, least of all to me.

"What I remember most was that I couldn't change my mental state. I didn't want to be depressed. I couldn't get out of bed in the morning even if I wanted to. And, here's the point. In the condition I was in, as sick as I was, there is no comparison between the depths of my illness and the mental problems your mother had. When I consider that I would have taken my own life if a cop hadn't come along, I can see, under the right mental conditions, how your mother could have done what she did. What I have heard so far has convinced me that your mother was ill. And I think I could make the argument that she was not responsible for what happened."

"But it happened, Jack." She drew my name out into two syllables.

"It was tragic. There wasn't anything anyone could do to change it." I scooted along the blanket until I was hip to hip with her. "I think the question you need to ask yourself is, 'If she was of sound mind, would she have done this?'"

"I think the question is broader than that. Can I forgive her for what she did? I'm angry, bitter and I've spent my entire life hating her. If I can't reconcile those feelings there is no point in meeting with her. And right now, I don't want to think about this anymore."

I said, "The only piece of the puzzle that we don't have is your mother's side of it. I don't think you'll have the why-it-happened until you have her input."

"Then you think I should meet with her?" There was an edge to her voice. It was obvious this was not what she wanted to hear from me.

"Yes, if only to have a complete picture."

"I don't want to think about this right now."

I slipped my arms around her, told her that I loved her and reassured her that I supported her in whatever decision she made. She let me hold her in silence and I could feel the tension of the day drain from the muscles in her back. She stretched out on the blanket on her stomach and asked me to put sunscreen on her back. I lay down beside her and tried to consider how she must feel, but I couldn't. Despite my own challenging past, and the events that led to my own depression, nothing in my experience could rise to the level of the events in her life. Nothing.

I knew enough that unresolved anger and bitterness sapped the spirit and ate away at peace of mind. Her hatred of her mother was an emotional cancer she could only exorcise through forgiveness. It concerned me that such a metastasis might hinder my relationship and intimacy with Jody.

I knew that I couldn't push her. She had to come to this point on her own. I was banking on my limited knowledge of Helen Holland. As a young man, she took an interest in my writing and helped me. It was a selfless act of kindness done without any possibility of recompense. She impressed me then as a giving and loving person. There was nothing about Helen Holland, at least the person that I met and interacted with, who could have perpetrated the crimes that she committed. Her departure from reality had to be an aberration. From everything that I had read in the files, Helen Holland had devoted herself to improve and enrich the lives of those around her. This behavior was consistent with the Helen I knew in 1961. If the psychosis she suffered was temporary, as Dr. Carnes had said and if that goodness and decency I saw in her was the driving force in her life, then I was confident that a reunion between mother and daughter would be beneficial.

First, Jody had an enormous heart and capacity to love. I couldn't imagine her visiting her mother and be oblivious to her mother's basic goodness. The writer in me could see the broad sweep of Helen's life and the tragedy the single event had created. I was certain that Jody would connect with her mother if only she would choose to meet with her.

Second, I was certain that if Helen Holland were the woman I thought she was, then she would be able to reach out to her daughter and connect with her. I remember she had the same people skills Jody had. They both made me feel important and special. I was hopeful that Helen could impart this feeling to her daughter.

But the circumstances of the reunion, and the height and breadth of the wall that stood between them was formidable. As hard as I tried, I couldn't walk in her emotional shoes.

Jody lay on the blanket with her head turned away from me. I reached out, took her hand in mine and interlaced my fingers with hers. She tightened her grip and released it. She lifted her head and turned toward me.

"I'm okay, Jack. I'm sorry I snapped at you."

"No need to apologize."

She closed her eyes and I searched her flawless face wishing I could lift the burden of her past from her. The rest of the afternoon passed in silence and I prayed that she would find some peace. That she could free her heart from the burdens she carried.

Eleven

"The Everglades is disappearing isn't it?" Jody looked out the passenger window as we aimed toward Florida City on the Florida Turnpike.

I said, "I remember as a kid you didn't have to drive far west of Hollywood to be right in the middle of it. Now, through dredging, and filling there isn't much left."

"Hollywood is the same way. When we were kids, it was a small town. Now look at it. From Miami to Palm Beach it all looks like one big city. Do you ever miss living here?"

I said, "No. I miss the memories of the place. The Hollywood I knew no longer exists."

"Nothing stays the same does it? We have so little control. You either roll with life or it runs you over." She looked at me with wide sunglasses over her thin face. She wore a short, pale yellow skirt and a white, loose-fitting sleeveless top. She scooted toward the middle of the bench seat, placed her hand on my thigh and gave me a pat.

I thought about Billie, my lost relationship with Em and the horrible things in Jody's life. "It sure seems that way doesn't it."

I wanted to change the subject away from the heaviness of her past with her mother.

"Tell me about your gallery."

"My husband Barry was a good provider, Jack. I was well cared for when he passed away. When the kids started school, I went back to school myself. First, I finished high school then went to the University of Georgia for a bachelor and master's degree. When I was an undergrad, I took some art class electives and loved it so much I took my master's in fine arts."

"You're an artist? You didn't tell me that."

"Yep. Oils. But it has been a long time since I have devoted any time to it."

"So how did you decide to open a gallery?"

"When I moved to Key West, I knew I couldn't just lie around on the beach all day, so I began to explore opportunities. I had thought about painting again and I investigated ways of selling my work. As I poked around town, I noticed all the local galleries were expensive–high end. At the other end of the spectrum, I couldn't find affordable art except at the periodic art shows on the Island. There were plenty of artists. They just needed an outlet. With tourists flooding the island, I sensed a real demand for reasonable priced art."

"Why Key West?"

"I went on a Caribbean cruise with Barry five years ago. Key West was one of the stops. I fell in love. It wasn't until after I moved to New Hampshire and experienced the bitter cold there, that I knew I wanted to settle down here."

"What possessed you to move to New Hampshire, of all places?"

"Barry and I had traveled through New England one summer and stayed at a bed and breakfast outside of Warner. I'm a hopeless romantic, Jack. As we traveled through the little town, I could imagine me living there with all the beauty of New England as subject matter for my art. After the funeral, I couldn't bear to live in our house in Georgia any longer. So I sold it and moved there. I still have the house. You would love it. During the summer, it is paradise. But, I was lonely. The kids were having a fit that I was so far away. I tried to get to know people there, but as friendly as they were, they weren't as welcoming as folks are here in Key West."

"What are you going to do with the house?"

"Sell it. It is already more work than I can handle or want. We should go there before I put it on the market. The romantic in me can see you in front of a typewriter by the fireplace." She giggled. "Do you even know how to use a typewriter anymore, Jack?" She smiled.

"For the longest time I couldn't write on anything but the old Smith-Corona my mother gave me. Now, I wouldn't trade the keyboard on my laptop for a million bucks. Hey, I'm modernized."

She patted my knee and chuckled.

I asked, "How do your kids feel about you living here?"

"They like it. They complain about the distance, but as long as I foot the bill for their airfare, they're good. It's a little cramped at the house of course, but we make do."

"So what did you do after you got out of school?"

"I didn't want the kids in daycare, so I stayed home. I kept busy with my painting and tried to sell my work at shows around Atlanta. Barry was a successful attorney, so I didn't have to work. Then Barry had a horrible car accident. He'd been out late at night with clients and they say he fell asleep behind the wheel. I think he'd had too much to drink. He had a bit of a problem with alcohol. He ran head-on into another car. My life has been in an uproar ever since."

"So tell me about the time before Barry."

"You already know it. I was a mess. I got involved in a convenience store robbery and received a two year suspended sentence. One of the conditions of my parole was to enter counseling. Barry worked that out."

"How was Barry involved?"

"He was my attorney. My aunt hired him. He was in his mid-thirties and partner in a good law firm. The officer, who arrested me, saw something in me that others didn't, and worked with Barry to keep me out jail. Barry and I fell in love – or I should say Barry fell in love with me."

"You didn't love him?"

"Jack, I was so messed up, I couldn't love anyone. But yes, in time, I fell in love with him. It was sometime after Barry Jr. was born before that happened."

"So tell me about the counseling. Did it help?"

"Some. It made me face some things. I had convinced myself that I could have stopped my mother from trying to kill us all if only I had . . . all you need to do is fill in the blank. I felt guilty that I had survived when all my siblings had died. I felt no one wanted me. After all, my mother tried to kill me. It didn't help that my aunt didn't want me around. She took me in because it was an obligation. Her heart wasn't in it. The fact that I was so difficult didn't help matters much."

"You said counseling helped some. What didn't it help?"

"I was so angry when I first married Barry. Thank God, Barry was patient and so loving. Through counseling, I learned to some extent not to blame myself, and that I couldn't have controlled the events that happened. I still feel guilty about it and I'm still not over the anger at my mother. But, you know that."

I regretted that our conversation had come full circle.

"Tell me more about Barry." I didn't want to press her feelings about her mother.

"Barry was ten years older than me. At the time I met Barry, I needed an anchor, someone to lean on; a father I hadn't had. He fell in love with me, he says, during his first visit to the county jail following my arrest. I needed love from someone. We started dating as soon as he made bail for me. He kept telling me that what he was doing–dating a client–was so unethical, but he said, he didn't care.

"He got me into counseling as part of a plea deal and got me off with a suspended sentence. Within three months, he asked me to marry him. And I did."

"How long were you in counseling?"

"About a year. That was tough. Hard work. A lot like what we're doing now, digging into my past and coming to terms with it."

"When was his accident?"

"Four years ago. So now, I get to ask some questions. How long were you married to Emily?

"Eight years.

"How did you meet?

"I needed an editor. I called the English Department at Stetson University to see if I could find a student who wanted to make some extra money. Em answered the phone."

"So she was a student? How old is she?"

"About forty now, eight years younger than me. She was a journalist not making a lot of money, so she went back to school to get a master's so she could teach. Instead she went to work for me."

"You were married before Emily," a statement, not a question.

"Yes."

"Well, tell me about it."

"Those were not my finest hours."

"Hey, you. I've been spilling my guts here for more than an hour. I want to hear about it." She punched me in the arm.

"Okay, already. I had just gotten out of the service."

"You were in the service? Vietnam War?"

"Yes."

"I didn't know that. Where did you go to school?"

"Didn't go to college. So strained was my relationship with my father, I enlisted in the service to get out of his house. I ended up in the Army National Guard and served two years active duty."

"Did you go to Vietnam?"

"No. I ended up in the Army as a technical writer working in the Pentagon."

"Is that where you met your first wife?"

I hadn't thought of those times in ages. And I didn't want to. The experiences of the summer of 1961 had a lingering effect. I was fifteen when *Lifetime Magazine* published my first short story. And with the magazine's help, I published my first novel shortly after I got out of the service. This should have been a time of great happiness. Looking back, I was missing something, searching for something and I thought marriage would solve the problem. It only made things worse. "Yes. We were both working at the Pentagon. She was from Iowa and it was her first time away from home. We were both lonely, needy and got married for all the wrong reasons."

"How long were you married?"

"Four years. Half of that time, we were in the Army Then we both got out and tried to make a living. Although my first novel was successful, the royalties were not enough to live on. To survive, we moved to Iowa to live with her parents, but I knew she wasn't happy and neither was I. Her parents viewed me as more a freeloader than writer, which created friction almost from the beginning. So I left her in Iowa, and came back to Florida alone. She finally filed for divorce. Again, not my finest hour."

"So you were what, twenty-four when you got divorced?"

"Yep. The only good thing to come from that time was the writing. By the time of the divorce, I had published two more books and I could support myself. It was a meager existence, but I could put groceries on the table."

"So you were single for fifteen years?"

"Yes. My need for solitude and my preoccupation with my work were incompatible with any meaningful relationships."

"You sound like you're quoting someone."

"Someones."

"Why were things with Emily different?"

"Emily was self-contained. She was self-assured and needed nothing more from me other than to feel loved. She understood me. She identified with my work. My work bound our careers. It was as much of a partnership as it was a relationship. We did fine until I started struggling with depression. I couldn't convince her that it had nothing to do with her. In the end, the partnership was not enough to keep our relationship afloat. I was sick and I pushed her away; drove her away, actually."

She withdrew her hand from my knee. There was silence as she, no doubt, processed what I had just told her. I could imagine her thinking about how things might go wrong between her and me.

She asked, "Do you think I'm needy, Jack."

"I think you're beautiful."

"So, you think I AM needy," she said, and slapped my knee.

"Jody, I don't know. I don't think so. But we haven't spent a lot of time together. Do you think you're needy, whatever needy means?"

"Could I survive a relationship when I knew that someone I loved didn't want to be with me? I don't think so. If that's needy, then I guess I fit the definition."

"Well, that's exactly what happened with Emily. Although I didn't mean to do it, I made her feel that way. As you get to know more about Em, I just want you to understand that it was not her fault."

"So . . . what will make things different between you and me?"

I had been dreading this conversation for several days. But, I knew that it was unavoidable. In a way, it pleased me that we'd finally made it to the crux of any future we might have together. The question was appropriate. Em struggled with the same question, "How do I know that this won't happen again?" Em was not willing to wager on a permanent recovery, and she knew me better than anyone did. Although I felt with everything in me that I had turned a permanent corner, my past actions were a much more reliable predictor of future behavior.

I said, "I wish I had a good answer for that. I feel like I have come to grips with my past and that I was able to move past it. Can I guarantee that it will never happen again? I don't think that would be fair to you. I was sick, and, during my illness, I did things and treated Emily in a way that I would have never done if I had been well."

She put her hand back on my knee. "That sounds like my mother, Jack."

I considered her observation. I thought to myself that my actions were the consequence of my skewed thinking. And when my thoughts were irrational, when they departed from reality, I did things and said things that were inconsistent with a sound mind.

I said, "That's a fair comparison. It is hard for me to confess to you that I was mentally sick. My thinking was as corrupt as a computer with a virus. I found the errors in my programming that caused the problem and now I feel better with each new day. But I can't promise you that it will never happen again."

"We're all broken, Jack. In some form or another, we all have problems. Perhaps that's where Emily and I are different. You and I have deep emotional scars. As a result, I don't handle rejection well. It would kill me to think that you didn't want to be with me anymore. But I'm willing to risk it. And I'm no prize either, I have enough baggage to start a shipping company," she giggled at her own joke.

"When the time is right, I want you to talk with Emily. I put her through hell. I want you to understand it in detail."

"I don't need to do that, Jack."

"You should. It's part of me. You should understand it."

"Like you getting involved with my mother?" Full disclosure?"

"Yes, something like that."

"Let's not talk of this anymore. I'm here and I'm not going anywhere." She slid closer to me on the seat of the SUV as we crested the top of the Seven-Mile-Bridge. The ribbon of concrete pointed south and split the shimmering, aquamarine waters. "I want to meet with my mother, Jack. But I don't want to meet her alone. Would you contact her and set it up?"

I told her I would. What would the two of them have to say after a separation of more than thirty-five years? And what I wanted to know, was how Jody's mother handled having five lives on her conscience for all this time?

Twelve

Key West

1996

It was lunchtime when we entered Key West. At The Mangrove, there was a long line, so we wended past the host station, through the courtyard and took two seats at the bar. I ordered a light beer and Jody a sweetened ice tea.

I left Jody at the bar and found my way into the kitchen. Billie assembled plates, matching them to paper orders hanging in front of her. She handed the plates to runners who dashed about the restaurant delivering meals.

I got her attention. "I just wanted to let you know Jody and I are here. We're at the bar."

"Give me a few minutes until the dust settles and I'll join you." Billie turned to one of the runners and said, "Tell Tonya to hold the next table for my brother and me." Turning to me, she said, "It'll be about ten minutes."

Jody was sipping iced tea, when I returned. I came up behind her, rubbed her shoulders then sat next to her. "Deep in thought?"

"I'm trying not to be. I was thinking about all the things you have on your plate right now: your publisher, Emily and dealing with my mom and me. You came here to rest. "

"I am, Jody. The only stressful event is meeting with Barksdale. I don't know why I let Emily set that up. I'll gain nothing from it. Emily wants the opportunity to tell him to buzz off in person. I would prefer to not see him at all."

"Then why did you agree to do it?"

"I guess information. I want to know what he's willing to pay to get me back."

"Why? It doesn't sound like you're interested in signing with him again."

"It's like getting an appraisal before you put your house up for sale. You need to know what it's worth. I want to know what Barksdale thinks I'm worth now that there is demand for my work."

"Are you ready to start writing again, Jack? Two books in ninety days; now that's pressure."

"Writing, Jody, is what I do. Yes, I need a break and I'm enjoying this one. In the end, though, it is something I have to do. When I couldn't write, it nearly killed me."

"Have you thought about your next book?"

"Yes. It is the story of you and your mother."

"I should have never asked you to do that. That was so unfair. I won't hold you to that." She swirled her drink with her finger, then sucked her finger dry.

"It is a compelling story, Jody. And we still have an ending to write."

"Yes, that scares me."

"What scares you?" Billie asked from behind us.

Jody answered, "Meeting my mom."

We both got off our stools and exchanged hugs with Billie.

To both of us Billie said, "Come with me, I've got a table for us."

I said, "I need to take care of the drinks."

"Your money is no good here."

We followed Billie to a table in the back of the courtyard near the main building.

"Sit. Sit." She pulled a chair out for Jody and pointed to a chair opposite for me. She sat between us.

Billie was particularly cheerful.

"Billie you're radiant."

"I'm so excited! We're going to have a party!" Billie bounced a fist off the top of the table.

"Party?" I asked.

"I told you, I'm having a lease burning party. I didn't want to do it until you and Jody were both here. On Monday, I'm closing the restaurant for the evening. I've invited friends, some of my best customers and of course you two."

"I'm so happy for you, Billie," Jody said. She reached across the table and gave her arm a squeeze.

"I'm going to let you guys in on a little secret. Alex doesn't think I handle money well. She took out personal loans and loans against the house to pay for improvements to the restaurant. Well, I paid off all those loans, thanks to the inheritance your father left me, Jack. I've repaid Alex, too. That's cause for celebration. It is like paying off a mortgage. It is like I'm free, like I don't have anything hanging over me or my restaurant."

The way Billie talked about freedom caught my attention. It wasn't so much the use of the word, but the force behind it. "Billie, I can't tell you how pleased I am."

My father was responsible for my estranged relationship with Billie. He treated her horribly when we were teens in Hollywood. He passed away recently and atoned for the atrocious way he treated her with a significant share of his estate. Her share was more than enough to pay cash for the restaurant and with enough left to pay off their debts. My father acted nobly. First, Billie was not his child. Billie was my mother's only child from her first marriage. Second, he'd thrown her out of his home when she was eighteen because he discovered she was a lesbian. The act caused irreparable harm to my mother's relationship with Billie. It did significant damage to my mother and father's relationship. The wound lay open for more than thirty years until my father had a near death, religious experience. He wrote Billie into his will just before he passed away.

"Why doesn't Alex think you can handle money? I asked.

"It isn't that I can't handle it, she thinks I can't handle the stress that comes with it. She says I obsess over it and that my energy is better spent making the restaurant a success." Billie raked her rusty red hair with her fingers. "Now, because of your father, I won't have that worry anymore."

"So who's coming to the party? Anyone I know?" Jody asked.

"Cynthia Pike, you know, the attorney who handled my lawsuit against my landlord? Several of the people from the Business Guild who helped when Coats shut the power off to the restaurant are coming. I invited all the employees of course and Mrs. Berger, my housekeeper."

Coats was Billie's previous landlord. He put the building up for sale then refused to sell it to Billie because she was a lesbian. He tried to evict her and harassed her constantly until Billie filed a lawsuit charging him with discrimination. She won and the court ordered Coats to sell the restaurant to Billie.

I said, "Come to think of it, I don't remember seeing Mrs. Berger the last time I was here."

"She was in Germany. One of her sisters passed away."

"I don't think she likes me much."

"Nonsense, she loves you. She's just a little rough around the edges."

Jody asked, "How are your plans coming to upgrade the restaurant?"

"I'm only upgrading the kitchen. It's outdated and, at the busiest time of the day, it's impossible to work in. I'm pleased with everything else. The chef hates the conditions. If I don't do something, she'll leave. I can't afford to lose her."

I asked. "So does this mean going back into debt again?"

"No. Without having to pay a lease and loan repayments, there should be enough cash flowing through the business to pay for it as we go. My chief worry is the chaos the construction will create."

A new voice chimed in. "What chaos are we talking about?"

Alexandra, Billie's partner, leaned over and kissed Billie on the cheek. Jody and I stood, but she demanded that we not. She went around the table and kissed Jody.

"Alex, I was just telling them about the problems it will create when they start tearing up the kitchen."

Alexandra was tall and thin, her long jet-black hair now up in a braid. Her peach colored top and white shorts a contrast to a deep tan and dark features.

"Tearing up the kitchen?" She asked as she sat between Jody and me and across from Billie.

"You know—the remodel?"

"This is the first I'm hearing of it." Alex looked at Jody and me, embarrassed.

"Well, I was telling Jody and Jack that the chef has been threatening to quit if we don't do something with the kitchen. So I got a kitchen designer to draw up some plans. The architect will reconfigure space in the main building to make it happen."

"And that couldn't wait until I got back from my trip?"

Billie glared at Alex, "Let's talk about this later."

Alex said, "Well, I have some good news to share. Another airline has purchased my airline. Rumors are flying about possible layoffs."

"Why?" I asked. "The economy is doing well. The last I heard, airplanes are full and the airlines are making a killing."

Alex said, "Well that news must have escaped the attention of our CEO. He has been too busy selling off the company's assets and running us into bankruptcy."

Billie said, "You have so much seniority. This won't affect you, will it?

Alex said, "I have seniority with my airline. I have none with the airline who acquired us. They bought us to gain routes they don't have. They can't fly into cities they want because there are no gates available at the airports. They have to buy our company to get the gates. We serve many of the same cities they do. Once the acquisition is complete, the crews who fly those duplicate routes will be surplus. And they sure as hell won't cut their own pilots."

"Still, you have enough seniority to survive that don't you?" Billie looked at Jody and me as though we could have given her some assurance.

"The union examined our overlapping routes. They project that we will lose forty-percent of the cities we serve. That means they could lay-off forty to forty-two percent of our pilots. I have seniority on forty-two percent of our pilots. That puts me right on the line. It is close. Too, close."

Jody asked, "Can't you just go to work for another airline?"

"If they lay off pilots, the market will be immediately glutted with talented people. Today, aviators who flew thousands of hours during the Gulf War can't find work."

"New airlines are starting up all the time," I said.

"Yes, but the new startups are nonunion and they pay next to nothing. I would have to move to Atlanta, or New York or one of their hubs. And they don't have flights to Key West. I would have to pay to commute from here to wherever they assign me. So I would have that cost on top of a sixty-percent cut in pay."

Billie asked, "When will you know?"

"I don't know. The FAA still has to approve the deal. Well, that's my big news. Now if we all had a drink, we could toast. Jack, you've just gone through a similar situation didn't you?"

"You mean my publisher sending me down the river without a paddle?"

"Yeah, Billie was telling me about it. How are you dealing with it?"

"At first, it was devastating. They handled most of my novels and they were all successful. My agent worried that we wouldn't find another publisher. As it turns out, this may have been one of the best things to happen to me. Emily, my manager, tells me we have several bids from other publishing houses. Reynolds and Ryan, the guys who fired me, are having second thoughts." I tried to think of something to say that would encourage Alex. "Maybe what is going on with your company will be a watershed event for you, too."

"I appreciate your optimism, Jack. But I'm nothing but a glorified bus-driver. The industry is going through a major transition following the deregulation of the airlines. Pilots who grew up during the seventies and eighties were all union and well paid. Competition forced the airlines to reduce cost and streamline their business. Now, veteran pilots are retiring. The airlines are squeezing their newer pilots for lower salaries and reduced benefits. Even technology is working against us. The new planes are smarter and more efficient. Soon they'll be able to fly themselves and one day they won't need pilots. The glory days of manned-aviation are over. It is downhill from here. A watershed event? I doubt it. I just hope I can survive long enough to retire."

"It will work out, Alex. Try not to worry," I said.

Billie said, "I need to prepare for dinner. Before I go, I want to hear about your and Jody's trip to Hollywood. What did you find out?"

Jody took the initiative and gave Alex and Billie a thumbnail of our trip. It was interesting to hear her perspective, the things she emphasized and the things she neglected to share. She talked in detail about the events that led up to her mother's release from the hospital. The fact that she was never prosecuted for her crimes. For Alex's benefit, she described what her mother had done to her family. She only vaguely referred to what her mother had done once she got out of the hospital. She mentioned that she'd become a doctor, but none of the humanitarian work she'd done on behalf of women suffering from PPP.

Billie asked me for my impressions of the trip. I filled in some but not all of the details Jody omitted. I didn't want Jody to feel that I was correcting her.

"I've decided that I am going to meet with my mom. I told Jack about my decision this morning."

No one spoke for a few moments. Then Billie asked, "Are you frightened?"

"Well, I guess I am. It makes me nervous. I have no idea what I'll say to her. 'Hi, mom. Let's talk about the day you tried to shoot me?'"

I said, "I don't think you need to worry about that. She's the one who wants to talk to you. Seems to me the onus is on her to shape the conversation."

"Well, anyway. I want to hear what she has to say."

Alex said, "What a horrible thing to have to relive. You're brave. I'm not so sure I could do it."

Billie stood up. "Jody, if we can help in any way. If you want to meet here at the restaurant, I can clear the private room in the main building."

Alex chimed in, "We'll do anything you need us to do, Jody. You name it."

"Thanks to both of you. You have been special friends to me. You don't know how much I appreciate it. I haven't contacted my mother yet. When I connect with her, I'll have a better idea of what I'm going to do."

Billie said that she needed to help the chef.

Billie stood and asked, "Are you going to stay at our house tonight? I'll need to let Mrs. Berger know."

"Let me talk with Jody and I'll let you know."

"Guys I have some errands to run." Alex hugged us both. "Good luck with your mother, Jody."

And things had come full circle again to Helen Holland.

Thirteen

I always thought Emily looked like a younger version of Jacklyn Smith. Not everyone saw the resemblance, but I thought she was a doppelganger. When she stepped through the jet way, it could have been a runway at a fashion show. She'd cut her thick light-brown hair to shoulder-length. Despite the strong breeze coursing through the jet-way, not a strand of her hair was out of place. She wore sparse makeup. A pale orange sleeveless dress, a single strand of pearls and white sandals highlighted her olive skin. As she approached, she pulled off her wide sunglasses and showed me a perfect toothy smile.

"Hi, Jack," she said and hugged me. She smelled of citrus and soap.

I hugged her back with more enthusiasm than I expected. "Hey, Em. It's good to see you."

She let me go, stood back a step, held me by the arms and searched my face, "How's it going?"

The question was about my not-so-recent bout with depression, the reason she divorced me, or so I thought. "I'm good," I said. I then added, "Excellent, in fact," for emphasis.

"That's great, Jack." She squeezed my arms, let me go, turned toward the terminal and began to walk. As soon as I was even with her, she slid her arm through mine and walked in step with me. "I have a lot of news to share with you, amazing news. I can't wait to tell you."

"How are you doing? You look terrific as usual."

"Thanks, Jack. You have always had the capacity to make me feel special. You haven't lost your touch." She squeezed my arm. "I'm doing well. I've been busy cleaning up your last novel. I just sent it off to R&R. And of course, I'm working with Lisa to find you another publisher. I haven't had much time to think about what we just went through."

She was referring to our recent two-month-old divorce. She told me that my multi-year bout with extreme depression had sapped her love. It also ruined a long-running partnership with my publisher. She said the split was one of self-defense, to save her from sliding into the same pit with me. The fact I had recovered was not enough to dissuade her from the divorce. It occurred to me as we walked to baggage-claim, that Helen Holland's and my situation were similar. She was mentally sick and in that sickness, harmed the people who loved her most. She didn't mean to do it, but it happened. One might argue that she'd nothing to do with it. That it was the result of some chemical imbalance in the brain over which she'd no control.

My psychosis may not have had chemical or hormonal origins, like Helen Holland's. But faulty emotional programming in my childhood led to an emotional meltdown that I was helpless to prevent. Was I at fault? No, I don't think so. Regardless of the circumstances and my state of mind, I set about to destroy my relationship with Em. I cut her off, isolated her and destroyed the love she had for me. What "we went through," was torturous to her.

"But you're doing well I hope?"

"Yes," she said, "and I've decided to move into the beach house."

The 'beach house' was an old rundown single-story oceanfront home in New Smyrna Beach.

"You always liked it there. It's a special place, isn't it?"

"Yes, it is. And I want to renovate it and make it my own. Thanks to your father, I have the money to do it right."

Em and my father were close. To her, he was a father figure and friend. My father's relationship with Em kept her sane when I submerged myself in darkness. My father never saw her as a daughter-in-law. He saw her as his daughter and treated her so in every respect. He made her an equal heir in his estate. My own dysfunctional relationship with my father had been a constant source of irritation to Em. I saw my father as an emotional terrorist, who did his best to destroy me, and succeeded. He was the virus sown into the emotional programming of my adolescence. My father's my-way-or-the-highway attitude left little room for me to take part in his life. I was his emotional punching bag, one that he practiced on my entire life.

Em saw my father as strong and self-sufficient. She extended grace when confronted with his insensitivities. She chalked them up to the veneer of a man's man. She lectured me often that I should be big enough to look past his boorish ways. That I should recognize that he loved me and only said the things he did to be of help. I felt that Em found qualities in my father that she felt I lacked, which made me resent my father even more.

"I'm glad you're remodeling and keeping it."

"How do you like it here in the Keys?"

"It has its own unique appeal."

"I can't wait to see it. Never been here," she said as she looked at the monitor in baggage claim to make sure she was in the right place. "From the air the aquamarine water was stunning. It looks like paradise."

"I'm sure Jimmy Buffet would be happy to hear that."

"I made reservations at the Pier House. Where are you staying?"

"I don't know yet. Either with Billie or a friend. Haven't decided."

"Who's your friend?"

"No one you would know. When is Lisa coming?" Lisa Catera was my literary agent. "I thought the two of you might come together?" I could tell she wanted to pursue the identity of my 'friend,' but she let it pass.

"She doesn't arrive until late this afternoon. I can't check into the hotel until three o'clock. They will not have rooms ready until then. I thought we would have lunch, come back to the airport, pick up Lisa, and then check in. You good with that?"

A warning horn sounded, the baggage carousel began to move and a worker loaded bags onto the machine. Em's were the first to come down the chute. She pointed out two large Hartman rolling bags and a smaller matching carry-on bag. "Planning to stay long, Em?"

"Stop." She gave me a love tap on the back, "A woman has to prepare for anything."

We each rolled a bag and I carried the small carry-on to short-term parking. Once in my SUV, I asked her, "What are you in the mood for?"

"When we were flying in, I noticed a Japanese steak house close to the airport. Could we go there?"

"Of course."

The restaurant butted up against airport property and was across the street from the ocean. We were early for lunch, so we sat in the waiting area on a teak slatted bench. As soon as they had enough patrons to fill a hibachi table, they escorted us to a u-shaped table that doubled as a grill.

The server came, lit the gas under the grill, took our drink orders and departed. We both ordered light beers.

"So what brought you down to Key West, Jack?"

"A lead on a story."

"What kind of story. You usually do your research on the Internet."

Although I hadn't planned to tell Em about Jody, it became obvious, I couldn't avoid it.

The server appeared with our drinks. It was a welcome space of time as I began to formulate how to explain Jody to Em. The young girl, dressed in a red kimono, took our food order. We both ordered Teriyaki chicken. Patrons began to file into the room, filling the remaining tables and adding their voices to the growing din.

We toasted each other and I waited for Em to take a sip of her drink before I began. "When I came to Key West in search of Billie six months ago, a woman I knew as a teen was a frequent guest at Billie's restaurant. Billie surprised me one of the nights that I was here and reconnected us."

"Reconnected you? How were you connected?"

I hated how perceptive she was. "I had a crush on her when we were kids."

"Childhood sweethearts, huh?"

"Something like that. Anyway, Jody was the oldest of five children. In 1961, her mother, who was responsible for getting my writing career off the ground, had just had her fifth child. Suffering from Postpartum Psychosis, she killed four of her children and her husband. She tried to kill Jody, but failed. Jody prevented her mother from taking her own life."

"That's horrible!"

"Jody's mother spent ten years in a mental hospital. The hospital released her in 1970. Jody and her mother haven't seen each other since 1961. A few weeks ago, a private investigator delivered a letter to Jody from her mother. It requested a meeting to reconnect. Jody has a few memories of what happened, but not many. She asked me to investigate before she made a decision about meeting with her."

"Why is she asking you to do this?"

"In 1961, three things happened that related to the depression that ruined our relationship."

"You told me about the awful things your father told you about you becoming a writer. And I suspect, Billie was another and this is the third?"

"Yes. Jody's mother was a freelance writer for Lifetime Magazine. My mother submitted . . ."

"Yes, you told me your mother entering you in a short story contest. But how was Jody's mother connected?"

"She read the short story, liked it and forwarded it on to the magazine. She used her connections to get the story published."

"And the rest is history, I get it. But how is this connected to your depression?"

"Helen Holland killed her family and tried to kill herself. She was a writer. Hemingway was a writer and killed himself. My father's constant warnings that I would end up the same way were at the base of most of my issues. I hated him for belittling my writing. And then, wham, Hemingway kills himself, and then a few weeks go by and Helen Holland kills her family and tries to kill herself. Then my dad had Billie thrown out of our home. These three stigmas provided a solid foundation for my depression."

The hibachi chef flipped knives, created volcanoes with onion rings and set fire to cooking-oil smiley-faces on top of the griddle. I should have been amused. But, at last, I had the opportunity to explain to Em the events that led to my meltdown. His antics were not helping.

"That still doesn't explain why you feel obligated to help this woman dig into her past."

"First, it isn't just her past. It is my past, too. It happened to her family, but it happened to me. I liked and respected Helen. She encouraged me to write and backed it up with action. Jody was the first girl I ever liked. Then all this happened. These events devastated Jody. They took Jody to the hospital to treat her for a superficial gunshot wound to the head. The hospital called her aunt in Atlanta to come care for her. She called me from the hospital to ask me to come and be with her before her aunt whisked her away. Em, it was awful. I was her friend and I couldn't help her.

"When I came to Key West looking for Billie, it was Jody who helped me get my head straight. She reminded me of my father's diatribes on my writing. She remembered Hemingway's suicide and my father's warning that, if I continued to write, I would suffer the same fate. Then Jody's mother, a writer, tried to kill herself. She helped me piece together what had happened to me in 1961. She helped me see the damage these events caused. She brought me back to a time and place when I enjoyed writing and assisted me in getting my footing."

Food dispensed by our knife-wielding chef, filled our plates. We managed to eat and talk.

"Tell me about, Jody," Em said, with her mouth half filled with food."

"What do you want to know?"

"Is she married?"

"No, her husband died a couple of years ago in a car accident."

"What does she do?"

"She owns an art gallery on Duval Street."

"Is she attractive?"

"Why are you asking me this, Em?"

"Are you seeing her?"

"What difference would it make? We're divorced."

She put her chopsticks on her plate and pushed it away. She scooted around on her chair until she faced me.

Her probing sounded like a jealous woman. I felt guilty admitting to her that I had an interest in someone else. The reality of that admission felt like betrayal.

"I haven't been honest with you either. There is something I need to tell you and I have been waiting for the appropriate time."

I took a long pull on the light beer. "Okay. Let's have it."

"I'm getting married soon."

"Soon?"

"Next week."

The news took my breath. "What?"

She didn't respond.

Em divorced me two months ago. There was no way she could have met someone and developed a marriage relationship in that short period. When she first told me she wanted a divorce, I asked her if there was someone else. She denied involvement with anyone.

"Who is it?"

"You're not going to like what I have to tell you, Jack."

Fourteen

"Who is it, Emily?"

"I've tried to tell you, but there never seemed to be a good time."

"Who is it, Emily?"

The rest of the patrons at the table turned toward us as I raised my voice.

"Shhh, Jack. Lower your voice." She whispered.

I thought about all the reasons wives take their husbands to public places to confess affairs. It was for just this situation.

"Who?"

"Bob Decker."

"What!" I bolted straight up from my chair. Now I had the attention of the entire room.

Em pulled my arm and tried to draw me back into my seat. I wasn't having it. I reached into my pocket, pulled out my car keys and a fold of bills. I tossed the keys on the table. I ripped off two twenties and dropped them in her lap. I pulled my arm from her grip and walked straight out of the dining room. I walked as fast as I could through the lobby and out into the bright sunlight. I walked past the parking lot, across the street to the sidewalk along the water. I wanted to be far away from Emily McNamara.

Bob Decker was my best friend, hell, my only friend. On occasion, we played golf together. We drank together when I needed to talk to someone other than Emily. He was my financial advisor . . . the son of a bitch. I trusted him; I believed in him.

And Emily. Through the divorce, she told me she didn't want to destroy our relationship. All that time she hid her affair with Decker. I was so concerned about fairness. I worked hard not to hurt her as we went through the process. I had already hurt her enough. I felt like a chump, as if she'd played me. My father mightn't have been so generous with his estate had he known of her infidelity. As I considered that, he would've blamed her indiscretion on me. He would have said 'I didn't deserve such a beautiful creature.'

I had been reluctant to step through boundaries with Jody. I had felt a sense of loyalty and honor to Emily. What seemed so noble at the time now seemed naïve. I had made it two or three blocks from the restaurant when I saw the nose of my SUV pull up beside me.

Emily rolled down the window and said, "Jack, we need to talk."

I didn't respond and kept walking.

"Jack, please. We need to work through this."

I didn't look at her but said, "I have no words for you, Emily."

"I don't want to leave it like this."

"Go back to the airport and catch a plane home."

"I'm not leaving until we work this out."

"We're done, Emily. If you have anything that belongs to me, leave it in the car. Go home."

"What about, Lisa?"

"That's no longer your concern. Now leave."

"I'm not going anywhere."

"Suit yourself. But I don't want to have anything else to do with you. Now leave before I lose my temper and I say things I'll regret."

She closed the window and drove off. I reversed course toward the airport to wait for Lisa. I just hoped Emily would take the next plane back to Orlando.

When I got back to the terminal, there was no sign of Emily. I checked the monitor and Lisa's flight was due in from Orlando in twenty minutes. Even the long walk back to the terminal didn't tamp down my anger. I was in no shape to meet Lisa. I was in no shape to be with anyone. So I hired a driver and limo to meet Lisa's flight and to take her to the Pier House.

I hired a cab to take me to the only place on the island I was certain not to see Emily again. I went to the White Street Pier.

The concrete structure jutted into aquamarine waters capped by the wind. Fishers of every color and age staked out spots along the pier, and made themselves at home. They brought coolers, folding chairs and umbrellas. They had fishing tackle of every description. From the most expensive Shimano reel, to a boy with a hand line and a red and white bobber, they lined the railing hoping for a bite. I claimed my spot at the end of the pier where the onshore breeze was constant. The sun, a white smudge against a clear pale blue sky, felt warm against my skin. Someone down the pier played reggae music. The volume drifted in and out with the intensity of the wind. When the wind abated, I smelled dead fish.

Yes, I was angry over Emily's betrayal. I was livid that Bob Decker, a valued friend, would violate that trust. My blood boiled over Emily's chicanery and secrecy through the divorce. Between my father's estate and her settlement with me, Emily became a millionaire, a woman of means. Her deception shattered my image of her as a woman of character. It all came down to the money. I felt so used – conned even. What made me most angry was that she conned my father. He was vulnerable and alone and she played him, too!

I thought about how often I wrote about love triangles. The plotting and scheming we humans can do given enough money, power or love was frequent subject matter in my novels. How could I have been so blind to the signs? How had she manipulated me so easily? I had written many times about the line between love and hate. The pure hatred I felt for Emily at this moment summoned adrenaline from every blood vessel in my body. My heart pounded in my chest. I felt the edges of darkness drawing me toward the abyss to which I had sworn I would never return. I closed my eyes, drew in as much air into my lungs as I could and let it out. With the salt air in my nostrils, and the breeze washing away at my face, my imagination took me to my childhood on Hollywood Beach. I remembered sitting at the water's edge, working through my father's abuse and the issues of our dysfunctional family.

I don't know how long I stood there, with my arms resting on the square rails of the pier. When I opened my eyes, there was someone leaning on the railing close to me. It was Billie. She didn't say anything. She just stood there looking out at the water.

"How long have you been standing here?"

"Not long."

"How did you find me?"

Billie's short red hair, driven by the breeze, looked like flames. "When you didn't meet your agent at the airport, we started looking for you. I figured you might be here."

"Emily found you."

"Yeah, she told me what happened and how upset you were."

"I don't want to talk about it."

"Alright." She continued to focus on the horizon. She said nothing.

"I'm not fit company for anyone, Billie."

"You don't have to talk, Jack, but I'm not leaving."

"I'm not going to talk about that bitch."

"I'm not asking you to."

She scooted closer to me, leaning on the rail. She squinted in the bright sunlight and watched pelicans dive-bomb for an afternoon snack.

I mentally tried to return to Hollywood Beach, but it was no good. Billie's presence anchored me in the present. She was a chock that kept me from sliding into the darkness. I turned toward her and she hugged me. She didn't say a word, she just held me.

After a considerable time passed she said, "You shouldn't be here alone. Come on," she pulled at my arm, "I'll buy you a drink."

Not having a better suggestion, I submitted to her leadership. I followed her to her crusty Volvo and sat in silence as we drove to her house.

We parked near Mel Fisher's and walked across the street to Billie's home.

Mrs. Berger met us at the door, stoic as ever. Though I know she remembered me, she greeted me as one would greet a vacuum cleaner salesperson at suppertime. Billie led me into the kitchen. She fetched a bottle of bourbon, two tumblers from the cabinet and some ice from the freezer. She poured liberal but equal amounts into the glasses set before us.

She sat on the stool next to me, "To better times than today!" We both took a healthy slug of the amber liquid. It burned on the way down but didn't quench the fire inside.

"Where are your things?"

"In my car, wherever that is?

"It's at the Pier House."

"Then I'm guessing Emily is still in town."

"That would be a yes." She took another sip from her glass, and swallowed hard.

"Did she explain what she did?"

"Yes, her side of it; and only enough to make me understand why you're so upset."

"Does Jody know?"

"Yes, the bare bones. When we couldn't find you, I had to call her to see if she knew where you were. Naturally, she wanted to know what was wrong. I should call her and let her know where you are."

"Can we hide for a bit?"

"For a bit. Jody is worried, Jack. I can't leave her hanging like that."

"You can call her in a few. Give me some time to pull it together."

I thought about the depth of my reaction to Emily's revelation of her affair with Decker. What was it that hit me so hard? It concerned me Jody would think I was still in love with Emily. That my emotional reaction would prove to her, I still loved her. I had to admit, despite my earlier confidence that I was over Emily McNamara, the crush I felt from her confession proved otherwise. Was it that I still loved her or was it the result of betrayal? Someone that I trusted with every corner of my life, deceived me, and not with some little white lie, it was so personal. Em was someone in whom I had confidence. No, it was more than that, I believed in her. She'd intertwined herself in both my professional and personal life. Trust was so fundamental to our relationship. That breach of trust, that deception, was at the base of my reaction.

"What did Emily tell you?"

"That she was marrying your best friend and that you took the news pretty hard."

"Did she tell you that she had been having an affair with him?'

"No, she didn't."

I took another hit on my drink; the elixir had already begun to work its magic. Then another sip. Then I drained the glass, and held up the tumbler for a refill. Billie poured mine, but refrained from adding to her glass.

I said, "Well I know Jody is going to want to hear what happened. I only want to explain this once, so maybe you'd better call her."

Billie picked up her cell phone from the countertop. She flipped it open and dialed Jody's number. She explained where we were and asked her to come.

"Are you okay?" she asked

"No, but if I have another drink like this I won't care."

"Better go easy. Emily said your publisher is in town and you're supposed to have dinner with him tonight."

"I thought that was tomorrow."

"She was adamant that I remind you. She made reservations at the restaurant at seven-thirty."

"Tonight?" I looked at my watch. It was three-fifteen. I panicked. I needed to talk to Lisa.

Mrs. Berger showed Jody to the kitchen.

"What's going on, Jack?" Her suntanned face wore lines of concern. She crossed the kitchen, slipped her arms around my waist and hugged me."

Billie said, "Let's sit at the table."

When Billie led us to the kitchen table, Mrs. Berger offered us iced tea to drink. We all sat and declined her offer and she departed.

I explained what happened at lunch with Emily. I covered all the nuances, the feeling of betrayal and skimmed the surface on the complications it created.

Jody said, "You're meeting with your ex-publisher at dinner? And Emily has been handling the negotiations with them?"

I said, "Lisa Catera has been involved, too. She has been pitching me to several other publishers. Emily has been handling Barksdale alone."

Billie said, "That makes things a little sticky, Jack. Can you handle the meeting tonight without her?"

I hated being in this position. I hated it that I had placed my trust in Emily. "Probably not. But I'm so angry at her for what she did; I'm not sure I could sit at the same table and concentrate on anything important."

Jody said, "Set your personal feelings aside for a moment. Has she proven untrustworthy with anything related to your business?"

"Until this morning I would have said no. Now, I don't know."

Jody said, "You said that she wanted to talk and that she wasn't going to leave town until you did. That sounds to me like someone who cares about what happens to you. She could have just hopped on a plane and left. She obviously doesn't need the money you pay her. You should talk to her, Jack, before dinner with Barksdale."

I hated the idea, but it made sense and it was the right thing to do. Once again, despite the hurt she continues to cause me, I still needed her . . . at least for tonight.

Billie said, "She's at the Pier House. I agree with Jody. You should talk to her."

Fifteen

The Pier House was a resort sitting on the most desirable piece of real estate in Key West. Enthroned at the end of Duval Street near Mallory Square, the grounds were tropical, the restaurant and bar top rate and the views of the ocean at sunset God-given.

The hallway outside of Jody's room was dark. After I knocked, the door sucked open and Emily was all business.

"Come in, Jack."

Without thinking about what to say I blurted out, "I'm angry with you, Emily. You've hurt me beyond words."

The dark brown colors in the room were mellow. Emily had littered her king-size bed with papers, and all the lights in the room were on. There was a small round oak table against one wall flanked by two casual chairs. Emily was not a drinker. But there were three empty minibar bottles of vodka standing guard over a tumbler half-filled with ice. "Drink?" she asked.

"Yes, as a matter of fact. I'll have what you're drinking."

"None left. I have some bourbon?"

"Good."

She filled a second glass with ice, retrieved a tiny bottle of Johnny Walker from the minibar, poured my drink and sat at the table. I sat down, took a sip from my drink and it burned in my throat with the same intensity as my anger.

"You've every right to be mad at me, Jack. I would say I'm sorry, but I respect you too much to offer you such a weak expression of my regret."

I bit my tongue. I knew that if I spoke now, I would spew venom.

She continued, "I wish I had a good explanation for what happened. Bob Decker was there for me when you walled me off. He helped me get through one of the most difficult times in my life, your rejection. Somewhere along the way, I fell in love with him. You were so sick and depressed. I didn't think you could handle the knowledge of my infidelity. When you came back from the Keys that first time, you'd started writing again. Your wounds were so tender and you were successfully fighting your depression. I just didn't have the heart to tell you the truth. There just wasn't a good time to tell you."

"You hid this from me during the divorce. You understood that if I knew about Decker, I wouldn't have been as generous in our settlement."

"Yes, I hid it from you, but not because of the settlement or the money. You had the threat of a lawsuit from Barksdale and two novels to write in less than ninety days. You had a divorce to go through on top of the beginning stages of a recovery from a devastating depression. Yes, I hid things from you to protect you. Let's talk about the settlement. Did I take advantage of you?"

"No."

"Did I ask for anything more than was fair?"

"No."

"Did I do anything to hurt you; to cause you harm?"

"No, but do you think my father would have been so generous with you, if he'd known about you and Decker?"

"He did know."

The revelation was stunning. My own father knew and didn't tell me. Then again, he'd been keeping secrets from me all my life. Why did it surprise me?

Em continued, "Bob Decker and your father were the only people I had to talk to when you crawled into that black hole of yours. Your father didn't like it, but he understood. He was the one who encouraged me not to tell you about it. First, he felt like things would change. That I would get over my anger with you and that we would patch things up. Then, you were in such a state; we both felt that you had enough challenges in your life. So, to address your issue, your father knew about it. He loved me, Jack, like a father."

"This is devastating." I looked at her. She was so calm, so matter-of-fact.

"Be honest with me, Jack. Be honest with yourself. If I had told you about this when I moved out, would you have been able to handle it?"

"No."

"When you came back from the Keys, you started writing again. You were under the gun. You needed to write or face terrible financial consequences. Would you have been able to handle the news then?"

"No."

"When we were going through the divorce . . ."

"Okay, Em, I got your point. No, I wouldn't have handled it well."

"Today, I felt like the time was right. You're doing better. I couldn't go through with marrying Bob without you knowing. I put it off as long as I could."

I hated that she was right and I hated that she knew me so well. "Of all the people in the world, why Bob Decker?"

"It just happened, Jack. You can't always choose who you fall in love with."

"But he's so much older than you."

"You and Jack are the same age."

I couldn't argue, but the betrayal stung. One thing was unmistakable. If there were still embers of love glowing for Emily, today's events doused them. I looked at the woman across from me whom I had loved and I felt nothing but bitterness."

We sat in silence. I picked a piece of imaginary lint from the knee of my pants as I placed mental salve on my wounded ego.

"Will you forgive me for what I did, Jack?"

I said, "I need time to process this. You've had months to think about all this." The saliva in my mouth tasted like metal. I didn't want to look at her. I had the right to be angry and I wanted to wallow in it.

"How are we going to handle, Barksdale? We meet with him in an hour."

"I don't know, Em."

"I've worked hard on this, Jack. I need to see this through. Can we set our differences aside for an hour? Let Lisa and me handle the meeting. Then I'll leave. Then you can decide whether we continue to work together or not."

"What about Lisa? She's handled Barksdale for a long time. Why can't she take care of it?"

"Because he has been talking with me, not Lisa. Lisa has focused on shopping you with other publishers. Let me handle the meeting. Let me finish this, Jack. I want this to go well."

"What is so crucial that you must handle it? I thought we were going to thumb our nose at him."

"I think he's eating crow right now for firing you. The response from other publishers has been stunning. Pre-sales of "The Tainted Lady," are at blockbuster levels and they're in love with the last novel we sent them. I think Barksdale will offer you more money and the flexibility to write anything you want."

"And, why do you think I'm interested in signing up for more of his royal arrogance?"

"Money. Switching publishers is a tricky business, Jack. You have a winning formula with R&R that has made them and you wealthy. Another publisher might not handle your work as well as R&R. We need to be open to what Barksdale has to say."

"Alright."

"Can I handle the meeting?"

"You can be there, but I'll handle Barksdale. After that, I need to think about where you and I go from here. What you can do now is find Lisa. I want to meet with both of you before we have dinner with Barksdale. Would you call Billie and see if we can meet at The Mangrove?"

"Billie already has a private room set up for the dinner. We can meet there until Barksdale arrives."

"Alright. I'll meet you at Billie's in thirty minutes."

"Jack. I'm so sorry this happened. I know you won't believe me when I tell you that I still care for you."

I got the keys from Em for my car, found it in the Pier House parking lot and decided to walk to Billie's rather than drive. With town so packed, this late in the day, I knew I wouldn't find a place to park near Billie's. So I retrieved my Hartman rollaway bag from my car and headed off to Billie's house.

April was the driest month of the year in Key West. Humidity hadn't yet descended on the Conk Republic. Daytime temperatures were still in the mid-eighties. The sun was white in a cloudless sky and an afternoon sea breeze whipped down Front Street. Emily's words, "I still care about you," echoed. Mother told me once that people who care are few and that I should count them as the true gemstones in life. I had found this to be true. Writing is solitary and isolated work and doesn't lend itself to making personal friendships. You have to be somewhat introverted to spend hours alone. So I tended to place a high value on the few friends I have. Em and Bob Decker were foundational relationships. I depended on them; no, I needed them, for emotional support. So their indiscretion was especially hurtful. As I walked past the Rooftop Café, I asked myself if I believed Em's statement of caring? I thought about how she stuck with me through the divorce. How she devoted herself to caring for my Aunt Ruby as she faced death. I had to conclude that her actions bore out her statement. As I tried to put my career back together after R&R dismissed me, she was still trying to help. She could have abandoned me, but she didn't. She stayed and the work she'd done had been outstanding. As I turned the corner off Front to Whitehead Street, I asked myself, "If she was trying to hurt me, then why did she stay?" It was not the money. With what my father had left her, she had no need to work. Our divorce settlement didn't entitle her to a share of any future books I wrote. What was her motive in meeting with Barksdale if not to be of help?

The four-story, red brick, Custom's House to my right stood resilient and under reconstruction. Built in the late 1890s, the historical structure was once home to the island's customs office, postal service and district courts. It stood behind a six-foot chain link fence to keep out vandals and the curious. I identified with the ongoing process to restore this unique architectural treasure. Since my own life fell into disrepair, I had undergone reconstruction and restoration. Circumstances had forced me to strip away the old and to remove all that's no longer valid. I have replaced old programs written into my psyche as a child with new ones. I have altered the thinking processes that made me so sick. The process has been painful, but character building comes at a heavy cost. When I think of the pain I have dealt with over the past six months, I don't regret it. I know these events are moving me toward something better.

When I arrived at Billie's, Mrs. Berger begrudgingly showed me to my room, and set towels out on my bed. I showered, shaved, dressed in light, gray slacks and a tropical short-sleeved shirt. I invited Jody to the meeting. I thought her analysis, afterwards, might be helpful. And maybe I wanted to show Jody off to Emily, to prove that I had moved on. Perhaps I needed a little emotional shoring up. As I walked to The Mangrove, I called Jody and asked her to join us.

A block away from the restaurant, Billie called on my cellphone.

"Barksdale is here early, Jack. He says he wants to talk with you before dinner. He says he brought four other people with him. Emily and Lisa are here and I just talked with Jody, she's on her way."

"I want to meet with Lisa and Emily before I talk with Barksdale."

"Alright, I'll buy him a drink at the bar. But he seemed keen on talking to you."

"He can wait."

Barksdale sat at the bar at The Mangrove with his back to me as I came through the entrance to the restaurant. In the private dining room, Billie had set up a rectangular table to accommodate ten people. Lisa and Emily huddled at the far corner of the table deep in discussion. The wait-staff had covered the table with white cloth and fresh cut flowers. Silverware wrapped in white cloth napkins and goblets filled with ice water covered the table. Billie knew how to set a stage.

Lisa broke off her conversation with Emily. She stood and walked around the table with outstretched arms. Lisa wore a pantsuit and her customary Reebok walking shoes. Her frosted hair hung straight to just below her ears. She never wore makeup, was professional, efficient and lacked pretention. She hugged me with enthusiasm.

She said, "Jack, this is long overdue." She broke our embrace, took two steps backward and appraised my appearance. "You look marbelous, daaling," doing a poor imitation of Billy Crystal, whom she worshiped.

"It's good to see you, too, Lisa." Under normal conditions, which haven't existed in a while, Lisa and I would talk every day. As much as it was possible for business associates to be friends, Lisa and I enjoyed a close relationship.

Lisa retraced her steps to her seat next to Emily and I joined them choosing to sit next to Lisa. Emily sat in the chair across the corner of the table.

I said, "Lisa, Emily tells me that you've some interest from other publishers. This would be a great time to tell me about them."

Lisa used a backpack like a purse. Hers sat at her feet and she removed a manila folder and laid it on the table. "The number of publishers interested in handling your work surprised me, Jack. I thought your public bouts with depression would hurt you in the market. I was wrong. R&R's release of "The Tainted Lady" and the rumors of your recovery have generated a lot of interest. In fact, it has worked in your favor. Five publishing houses can match your old deal with R&R. Of the five, only two would agree to handle books in a different genre. Hampton House and Mega Publishing are the two proposals I think we should consider. Hampton House has the best proposal. They're offering a onetime, half-a-million signing-bonus. They will also advance you one-million per book upon delivery of a completed rough draft. They will handle all the pre-publication activities including editing. They want you to deliver six Dana O'Brien series books in three years. If you fail to deliver, you will repay half of the signing bonus. In the next two years, they will pay half-a-million for two books in a new genre, pending their approval of subject matter. At the end of the two years, and depending on the sales of those new books, they will renegotiate the contract amount."

"And Mega Publishing?"

"They're offering something similar. No signing bonus and less for books outside the O'Brien series. They compensate by offering one-point-two-million upon delivery of a draft. You handle editing out of your pocket. They propose, on the new genre efforts, to cut you in for a larger portion of book profits. There is less up front, but if the books are successful, you will make more on the back end. They only want to handle one new genre book at a time. They stress that they're interested in looking at anything you want to write. But they want to risk-share with you until you prove there is a market for it."

"What is your recommendation, Lisa?"

"Jack, either deal is phenomenal. The Hampton deal is the better of the two. You have more income guaranteed and less risk, plus you get to spread your wings and try something new. I like the folks at Hampton. Three of my clients have deals with them. They're marvelous to work with as long as you live up to your end of the deal."

"I noticed that neither of these proposals offers a multiple book advance like I had with R&R."

"The consequence of your past illness, I'm afraid. If R&R offers a package like that again, that will surprise me. And do you want the pressure of that kind of a deal again?"

"No. I don't.

I said, "Emily, what do you think?"

"I think Barksdale is peeing all over himself about the prospect of you signing with one of his competitors. They have no one with the star-power you brought them. He acknowledged he screwed up. I don't know if his proposal will compare to the offers Lisa has, but I think you should hear him out."

To Emily I asked, "Why does he want to see me before the meeting?"

"I suspect he has some humble pie to eat, and he would rather eat it in private and not in front of his lawyers."

"He brought lawyers with him?"

Emily said, "He came here to do a deal, Jack. He wanted you to know that he's serious and to prove his determination, he came prepared to do whatever to win you back." She paused for a moment, "You're in a marvelous position. You have leverage. The question is how would you like to play this?"

"You think I should stay with R&R?"

"We haven't heard his deal yet. As I said earlier, he's the devil you know. You have a great record of accomplishment with R&R. The other offers are good, but you don't have any experience with them. They're the devil you don't know.

"Lisa?"

"I agree with Emily, we should hear what Barksdale has to offer. I do have experience with Hampton House. I think you would be happy there. In the end, though, you have to be comfortable."

"Alright, then let's do this. I don't want to meet with Barksdale before dinner. Let's suggest that he leave his attorneys out of our dinner meeting. They don't need to be there unless we accept his offer, which I'm not inclined to do. If he has any humble pie to eat, I want him to eat it in front of all of us."

As I stood to conclude the meeting, Jody stood at the door. "Lisa and Em, I would like to introduce you to Jody Holland."

Jody was stunning. Her blond hair hung down across her shoulders and her tanned face glowed. She wore whites and yellows and her blue eyes danced.

I was proud of how Jody handled herself. She was gracious and exchanged pleasantries with Lisa and Emily. I asked Emily to find Barksdale and escort him, sans attorneys, to our room. Lisa busied herself straightening up the table and Jody moved closer to me, took my hand and gave it a squeeze.

Sixteen

Nathan Aldous Barksdale III sauntered through the door to the private dining room at The Mangrove. His gray Armani Suit cloaked his inflated body and his diamond cuff links twinkled as he extended a manicured hand to me. Every square inch of Barksdale spoke of the money and the privilege of his lineage. His coiffed black hair and silver sideburns gave him a presidential appearance. His puffy jowls quacked as he shook my hand.

"Jack!" his voice boomed in the small room. "It is so good to see you."

"Right," I said to myself and shook his hand without comment.

Emily stood beside Barksdale as he moved past me and greeted Lisa. "Lisa, as always, you look wonderful."

I said, "Nate, (he hated me calling him that) this is my friend, Jody."

Barksdale said, "Hi, Jody." He extended fingers to Jody for her to shake, as the Pope might extend a ring for her to kiss.

"Why don't we sit," Emily escorted Barksdale to a solitary spot on the opposite side of the table from the four of us.

Barksdale said to no one in particular, "I just finished reading the draft of "Left Behind" on the flight down." Then he patronized me with, "Jack, it's your best so far." "Left Behind," was the title Emily came up with after her first read.

I saw this as empty praise since he said this at the completion of every book I wrote. I wanted to know the current state of R&R. I asked, "Beside *The Tainted Lady* and *Left Behind*, what other new releases do you have coming out next year?"

R&R was a top ten publishing house in New York. Barksdale had a stable of fiction writers and a decent pipeline of non-fiction books. He bloviated about current and near term projects. Nothing he mentioned rose to the level of a bestseller, nothing that would create profits. A significant portion of their bottom-line came from my novels and related movie rights. After he exhausted himself on how wonderful things were at R&R, it was clear they had a huge revenue crater and no author to fill it.

Billie's staff brought drinks, appetizers and a four-course, surf and turf meal. Barksdale had never been much at small talk. Beyond work, he had few interests. After his state-of-the-company talk, conversation dwindled. Lisa waxed about the rocky financial state of big-box bookstores on which R&R was so dependent.

We finished eating, the staff cleared dishes and served after dinner drinks. I said, "Nate, what brings you to Key West."

"I want you back at R&R."

"You just fired me, Nate."

"Yes, Jack. That was unfortunate, but I want you to know that I wasn't behind it. That was the board's doing."

Bullshit. "How did that go, you said their attitude was, 'what have I done for them lately.'"

Barksdale addressed all of us. "R&R is a public company. The company's price per share dictates the board's personal wealth. Jack, you failed to perform. The public nature of your debilitating depression sent R&R stock plummeting. The board was afraid if they did nothing, stock prices would collapse. Fear and greed drive my board. In a fearful panic, they decided you had to go. What they didn't count on was the analyst downgrades of our stock. Your leaving became a huge negative. When rumors surfaced that Hampton and Mega were pursuing you, the value of our stock went down even more."

"You could have stood up for me Nate. But you bailed."

Barksdale held up his hands, "Whoa, I didn't bail out on you. The board gave me a choice; I fired you or they fired me. When you went dark for all those months, you put us in a tough spot. We should have stuck it out with you. We should have intervened and gotten you help. There are many things we should have done and could have done. But canceling the contract was not one of them. It isn't easy for me to admit this, but I mishandled the whole thing, with both you and the board."

"What do you suggest?"

"Jack, I came here with a blank piece of paper and attorneys who can write an agreement. I'm wide open to anything that makes business sense. We both have to win, obviously. We made a dreadful mistake and I'm here to rectify it. We've had a successful business partnership for many years. You're doing better and your last two books have proven that you haven't lost your edge. I could give you a proposal, but I think it would be a waste of time until we decide if we can patch things up. I just want you to know I'm willing. The question is can you forgive us for what happened?"

I looked at Barksdale trying to read his pudgy pale face. Despite my desire to the contrary, I knew enough about him to know that there was no personal relationship here. This was purely business. If I learned anything, it is that professional loyalty has the length of a dollar bill. It was a romantic notion that Hampton, Mega or any other publisher would offer more than a pure business arrangement. Barksdale was right; we'd been successful. They had the right distribution channels. They had connections in the motion picture business to give my work maximum exposure. Yes, I was angry, and I felt betrayal from all quarters. In the end, just like the board at R&R, it was business and I needed to put my emotions aside.

"Nate, what percentage of R&R stock do you own?"

"That's confidential."

"I can get a Form 10K and find out on my own."

"Alright, four and a half percent."

"And if the board fired you, what is the amount of your golden parachute?

"Jack, I don't see what that has to do with anything?"

"Come on, Nate. I can make three or four phone calls and find out."

"Two years compensation equal to salary and bonuses."

"How much is that Nate?"

He adjusted his necktie, "About five million."

"What percentage of R&R's annual revenue do my books comprise?"

"Under normal circumstances, it ranges between eight and ten percent."

I looked at Lisa, then Emily. I should have broken off the meeting and huddled with them to get their input. The sting of Emily's revelation was still fresh and it emboldened me.

"There is nothing to forgive, Nate. You, the board, all of you did what was in your own interests. This is business. We all have to make money and I have to do what is best for me. I'll deliver . . ."

Lisa jumped in and said, "Jack, this is something that we should discuss in private first."

I ignored her, "I'll deliver six Dana O'Brien novels over the next three years, two each year. Upon completion of each rough draft, you will pay me a non-refundable advance on royalties of a million dollars. Over the next three years, you will purchase three books in any genre or subject matter of my choosing. On those books, you will pay me a nonrefundable advance of three-hundred-thousand. You will handle all the editing subject to my approval of the final draft. At the end of the three years, we renegotiate compensation. If you or the board decides to terminate the agreement early, then you will pay me a penalty of two-million dollars."

Barksdale was nodding and making notes as I ticked off the terms so far.

"Nate, I have proposals from Mega and Hampton for more than I'm suggesting here. As a signing bonus, I want three-percent of R&R's stock. In the future, if we fail to renew our agreement, I want the company to buy back any remaining shares of stock."

"Jack, I can't do that," he blustered.

"And . . . I want a voting seat on the board. This way we all have skin in the game."

"Jack, I don't even have a seat on the board."

I looked over at Lisa, and her mouth was agape.

"That's what I want, Nate."

Barksdale looked at Lisa, and Lisa shrugged her shoulders. He looked at Emily.

"You wanted to know what it would take to put the relationship back together," Emily said. "Now you know. I have contracts from Hampton and Mega right here ready for Jack to sign."

I said, "Nate, you should huddle with your board and talk it over."

"I'll have to. I'm not authorized to be that generous and it is too late in the evening to pull a board meeting together."

"Can you give me an answer by noon tomorrow?"

"Yes, but I'm not optimistic." Barksdale looked crestfallen.

I stood up. Jody, Emily and Lisa followed suit.

"Until tomorrow morning then."

Barksdale pushed himself up from the table as though under a great weight. He looked at me with eyes that hovered between anger and bewilderment. "Good night, Jack. I'll call Emily when we're ready to meet."

When Barksdale swaggered out of the private room, we all collapsed into our respective chairs.

"That was brilliantly played, Jack," Emily said. "Did you see him squirm when you said you wanted a board seat, I thought he was going to stroke out."

Lisa asked, "Why is that so important, Jack?"

I responded, "If that's where they make decisions about my future, I want to be there to influence them."

"Do you care about the internal workings of R&R? The stock I can see. That's one helluva royalty. If your books do well, it will show up in the value of the stock. The board will be a pain in your ass. That will be a giant distraction."

"Lisa, if it becomes a problem I can always resign. The board fired me. The board seat is a measurement of how badly the board wants me back. It is the only stick I have long enough to poke them in the eye."

Lisa said, "If they don't go for it?"

"Hampton's offer sounds good to me."

Lisa said, "Just like that?"

"Yep."

"Jody, what's your reaction?" I asked.

"It has to make you feel good, that people love the work you do."

I said, "It is feeling better all the time."

Lisa said, "I'd love to be a fly on the wall in Barksdale's room. What do you think the answer will be, Jack?"

"It doesn't matter. Thanks to the work you and Emily have done, it appears that I still have a career doing what I love to do. And someone will pay me well to do it. Either way, it works out; you both have made it a winning situation. Thank you.

Seventeen

By the time the meeting with Barksdale broke up, it was eight o'clock. As exhilarating as it had been, it drained me. I walked Jody home, kissed her goodnight and before I left her porch, she asked me again to call her mother and to set up a meeting.

I walked to the Pier House, got the rest of my things out of my SUV and left the keys for Emily at the front desk. She wanted to hang around until we heard from Barksdale, so I left her my wheels.

At Billie's, Mrs. Berger was gone, Billie was still at the restaurant and Alex was not there. So I went up to my room, changed into my pajama's and ascended the stairs to the attic, then up to the widow's walk on the roof. I flipped open my cellphone.

"Hello?" The voice brought me back to 1961."

"Hi, Helen. This is Jack McNamara."

"Oh my goodness. Jackie is that you?"

"Yes, Helen. Jody got your letter and asked me to call you."

"Oh, Jackie, I was so worried that I wouldn't hear from her. How is she doing? I worry about her, so."

Her voice was as gracious as I had remembered.

She asked, "Are you in Key West, too?"

"I'm just visiting for a while. I just finished a book and Billie and Jody invited me to come here for some vacation."

"Billie? That's your sister, right?"

"Yes, you have a marvelous memory."

"Yes, it is too good at times. What was Jody's reaction to my note? I was hoping that she would be receptive to seeing me."

"She wants to meet, Helen. She asked me to call and set it up."

"She didn't want to call me?"

"She's just being cautious. I'm sure you understand."

She was silent for a few moments then said, "She's still angry." She made a statement rather than ask a question.

"Yes, but I'm encouraged that she has agreed to see you."

"When do you want me to come?"

"You've a window of opportunity, Helen. I don't know how long it will be open. It depends on your schedule."

"There is nothing more important on my schedule. How about the day after tomorrow? Saturday? I could fly into Key West tomorrow evening."

It occurred to me that the finale to the Conch Republic Independence Day Celebration was this weekend. A weeklong event, it commemorated the faux declaration of independence by the Republic on April 23, 1982. Hotel rooms on the island would be hard to find.

"Do you want me to make reservations for you?"

"No, but thank you. I can handle it."

I explained the festivities this weekend, but she insisted that she was resourceful and would find a room.

She said, "I do have a question for you before we get off the phone."

"Shoot."

"Jody trusts you or she would have called herself. Where do I stand with you?"

"You mean, how do I feel about you coming?"

"No. You said Jody is still angry. What are your feelings toward me?"

"Confused and conflicted are two words that immediately come to mind. On one hand, I owe you my career, Helen. You helped me in a way that no one in my life has duplicated. On the other, your actions repulse me. What happened to your family, because of what you did was unspeakable. The trauma you inflicted on Jody was horrendous. My revulsive feelings will be hard to erase, regardless of how you explain away what happened."

"Thank you, Jack, for being honest. One more question and we will talk more when I get there. You said there was a window of opportunity with Jody. What about you? Are you open to hear me out?"

"If you'd asked me that question a week ago, I would've said no. Because of you and Jody, I'm learning and understanding more about Postpartum Disorders. The bridge between understanding and accepting is long, Helen. Am I open to hear from you? Of course."

Helen said, "I couldn't ask for anything more."

As I closed my flip-phone, I considered the enormity of the emotional issues that separated Helen and Jody. They were overwhelming. It was inconceivable Jody could both forgive and forget something that had almost crushed her.

"There you are. When I went to your room to look for you, I noticed the door to the attic was open. I figured you were up here."

"Alex!" I put my phone in my pocket, put my arms around her and hugged her. "We haven't had much of an opportunity to see one another." She looked as attractive as ever. She wore her long dark hair down. Her white, knee length shorts hugged her slim body and a sleeveless white blouse looked crisp against her olive skin.

"I've been deep into the airline buyout and helping the union plan for meetings with the new owners. The more I dig into the merger it looks like I'll be safe from any layoffs. Since the airline announced the merger, many senior pilots have bailed out. They either retired or found work elsewhere. I'm no longer threatened."

"That's wonderful news, Alex."

She looked at me and started to speak.

"What's up, Alex?"

"I need to talk to you about, Billie."

"Is everything okay?"

She turned and looked out over Mel Fisher's Maritime Museum toward a cruise ship parked at the dock. I followed suit.

"This conversation is between you and me, okay? I need your help."

"Alright. This is between us."

She rubbed her hands together. "Ever since Billie got that money from your father's estate, she has been a different person." She looked sideways at me as though judging my reaction. When I didn't say anything, she continued. "She treats me like she doesn't need me anymore."

"Have you talked to her about it?"

"I haven't had the opportunity. It's like she's avoiding me."

"She seems pretty busy right now and my being here isn't helping either."

"Jack, she's always busy. That restaurant is her life, but this is different. It is as though she has declared her independence from me. I'm beginning to feel a little used, like she needed me when she didn't have a dime to her name, but now . . ."

"I'm sure that isn't it. I know she loves you, Alex."

"Before she got that money from your dad, I would never have questioned that. But money has a way of changing things, Jack."

"How can I help?" I turned to face her.

She stood straight, with her hands still on the rail, still facing the waterfront. "How would you feel about talking to her about it?"

"If I talk to her about it, she'll know we've been talking about her."

"Couldn't you just feel her out about the money? You don't have to mention me at all."

"Billie's pretty perceptive, Alex. Don't you think it would be better if you just asked her about it?"

"Would you please do this for me? Would you please talk with her? You're the wordsmith. I'm sure you can find some way to bring the subject up without implicating me.

I don't want to cause a problem with her if there isn't one there."

"Alright. I'll talk with her."

"Thanks, Jack. I'm bushed. I'm going to bed. Billie called a few minutes ago. She said they were busy. She said the restaurant was "in the weeds," as she likes to call it, and that she would be late." Alex gave me a hug and headed for the door to the attic.

I turned back toward the waterfront alone with my thoughts. I pondered how I managed to get in the middle of so many relationships. I wondered if Barksdale was contrite enough to accept my terms. I mused about the impossible situation with Jody and her mother, and the monumental emotions Jody had to deal with

I worried about Billie. Did my Father's generosity have unintended consequences? Could his money have bruised Billie and Alex's relationship?

The most troublesome issue, to me, was whether to continue to employ Emily? What I had appreciated about her for eight years was that her strengths dovetailed with my weaknesses. Together we were a good team. When I considered the prospect of not having her around, I had to face my own professional inadequacies. She was still an attractive alternative to finding someone to replace her. This I rationalized in my head. She'd deceived me, and I was still angry about it. If I had to make an immediate decision, I would have fired her. As I watched an inebriated man stagger past Billie's home, on his way toward his cruise ship, I decided not to decide. I would leave the situation as it was for a time. There were too many emotional issues vying for my attention.

Eighteen

At nine-thirty, I was nowhere near sleep. I got dressed, descended the back stairs to the kitchen and met Billie coming up the back steps. She carried grocery bags, her face looked haggard and she seemed to struggle to find the energy to make it up the stairs from the yard into the kitchen.

"Oh, you startled me," she said when she looked up and almost dropped her bags.

"I'm so sorry, Billie. I'm headed to Jody's to see if she's still up. Here, let me help you." I grabbed the bags from her arms and followed her back up the stairs into the kitchen.

Billie flipped on ceiling lights and pointed to the counter top where she wanted me to put the bags.

"I just saw her ten minutes ago. She came by the restaurant for a late dessert. She left when I did."

"What about your day?"

"The Conch Republic Independence Celebration isn't a huge event. But the Conchs don't need much of an excuse to party and tonight, they were in the mood. They sucked the bar dry. I'm out of everything. I don't know how I'm going to handle lunch tomorrow. You had a pretty busy day I hear."

"Jody filled you in?"

"Yeah. She said you pinned Barksdale's ears to the wall."

"I hardly did that, but I did put a high hurdle in front of him to get me under contract again. I have a favor to ask."

"I'm listening," she said. She pulled items from the grocery bags and put them away in the cabinets and refrigerator.

"I haven't told Jody yet, but her mother is flying in tomorrow night and wants to meet with her on Saturday. Could we use the private room again?"

"Emily came by the restaurant earlier and asked me to reserve it tomorrow morning for brunch. Another meeting with Barksdale, she said."

"She didn't mention that to me."

"The room for Saturday is fine. Pretty soon I'm going to name that room after you." She smiled. "If you're going to catch Jody, you'd better get moving. She said she was heading home and hitting the sack."

When I left Billie, I approached Simonton by way of Front Street. Music blared from the Hogs Breathe Saloon one of Key West's most refined venues. Folks strolled in the balmy evening air near Mallory Square. One street performer, panhandling for tips, played blues on a sax. The throaty tones echoed off the buildings near Duval Street. A westerly sea breeze whipped through the parking lot at the Pier House. The wind jostled palm fronds and gave flight to errant handbills and tour maps discarded by tourists onto the street.

Simonton Street was quiet, and dappled by light from street lamps shining down through the trees. At her house, the lights were on, so I took the two steps from the street to her porch, and knocked on the door.

When the door opened, she had dressed in an extra-large, white men's tee shirt that gobbled her up and hung to her knees. "I was hoping that was you. I was just settling in." She waved an arm toward the living area. "Come."

Once inside, there was a clear wine glass sitting on a candle lit kitchen table. She said, "I just poured myself some wine. Can I get you some?"

I nodded, and took the other side of the table and sat. As I watched her pour my glass, I thought I had never seen a man's tee shirt look so appealing.

When she returned my glass to the table, she walked to my side, bent over and kissed me with enthusiasm.

She said, "I've wanted to do that all day. I wanted to do more than that when you were laying out your terms to Barksdale. But you were too busy at the time." She smiled, placed her cool palm on my cheek, then moved back to her side of the table and sat down.

"I talked to your mom about an hour ago."

The light disappeared from her face, like a cloud sliding in front of a full moon. "You know how to get a girl in the mood."

I said, "You asked me to call her. She'll be here tomorrow night."

"Tomorrow night?" She started to look around her small home in a near state of panic.

"Not here, Jody. I asked Billie if we could use the private room at the restaurant."

She sat back against the chair, a look of relief on her face. "I know I asked you to call her, but tomorrow?"

"Do you remember when we were kids in Hollywood? Billie set up a meeting between you and me at the ice cream shop near the Casino Pool. That was the same day she introduced herself to you."

She nodded, just a hint of a smile returned to the corners of her mouth.

I said, "When she told me what she'd done, I panicked. Just like you're doing now. You know what she said to me when I yelled at her for moving so fast?"

"You yelled at her?" She giggled, "I give. What did she say?"

"She said that if she'd delayed the meeting any longer, I would have worried myself sick about what to say to you."

The smile on her face broadened.

I said, "I remember that day like it was yesterday . . . and she was right. If I had scheduled it for next week, you would have worried yourself sick."

"Tell me about your conversation."

While I went over the details of her meeting with her mother, she began to undo the braid that bound her long hair. When she'd finished, she combed through her hair with her fingers, pulling it straight in front of her shoulders. The sensuality of the act was distracting. I couldn't concentrate on what I was saying. I stopped mid-sentence and just delighted in the effect she had on me.

She got up from her chair, walked around to my side, pulled my legs out from under the table and then sat in my lap. With her long hair hanging in my face, she kissed me once more. The heat of that moment melted away the worries of the day and the concerns for tomorrow.

Nineteen

The next morning, as I left Jody's on my way to Billie's, Emily called me on my cellphone. She'd agreed to a ten-thirty meeting at The Mangrove with Barksdale. Barksdale hadn't responded to my demands, but she said he'd been working all night on a response.

At Billie's, I showered and changed into casual attire. When I came downstairs to the kitchen, Alex had poured some coffee and offered me a cup.

"Sure," I said.

Alex wore her captain's uniform.

"Where are you headed?"

"Just a quick trip to Atlanta. The airline purchased some new planes and I have to put some time in on a flight-simulator. Did you get a chance to talk to Billie yet?"

"You want me to be discreet, right? So I'll have to wait for the right time."

"There is definitely something going on. She was rude to me this morning. I know there is nothing bothering her; heck, she doesn't have a care in the world . . . now. I found out from one of our friends that she's having a lease burning party. She never said a word to me about it."

"That does seem strange," I said. "I've got an important meeting this morning. This afternoon, I'll try to have a talk with her."

"Call me after you talk with her, will you?"

Alex put cream and sweetener in my coffee, handed it to me and said, "I gotta run. I'm late as it is and they'll not hold the flight to Atlanta for me." She kissed me on the cheek. "Bye."

As she left, her perfume filled the air, but the mystery of Billie's odd behavior remained.

The Conch Republic Independence Day Celebration made me feel that Key West really had seceded from the union. Partiers clogged Duval Street even at this early hour. At Billie's restaurant, the line to get a table stretched down Duval for half a block.

I found Lisa and Emily making preparations in the private dining room for our meeting with Barksdale. Gone were the accoutrements of yesterday except for the white tablecloth.

"Heard from Barksdale yet?" I asked to no one in particular.

Lisa said, "He called me this morning. He wanted to know how much wiggle room he had with your demands. Since you didn't discuss any of this with me in advance, I had to tell him that I had no clue." There was no disguising the edge in her voice. My go-it-alone approach yesterday had bruised her, a malady I needed to repair.

"Lisa, I'm sorry. A part of me wanted a pound of his flesh. He made this personal when he fired me. He didn't involve you when he did that. I wanted the opportunity to return the favor. It had nothing to do with you."

"Jack, if you'd given me some warning. I would have had a better opportunity to structure something, to refine your demands. Like this morning. Barksdale was looking for guidance. I couldn't help him. That's what agents do, Jack. That's my job!" She slapped a file folder down on the table. "Now, we're going into an important meeting ill-prepared. I don't like the feeling, Jack. It sounds like you don't trust me."

I looked at Emily, dressed to the nines. She shrugged her shoulders, stared at me for a moment, then busied herself fussing with a wrinkle in the tablecloth.

"Let's see what he says, Lisa. This may be much ado about nothing."

"It isn't nothing. It isn't just your future, either. I have a stake in this, too."

Billie made an appearance at the door. She said she had water and glasses coming. She asked Emily if she needed anything else. Emily shook her head and Billie backtracked to the kitchen.

Lisa continued, "So if Barksdale agrees to any of this, have you decided to return to R&R?"

"Depends on what he says."

"You're giving this serious consideration, then?"

"We're getting ahead of ourselves. He may not go for any of it."

"I hope you know what you're doing, Jack. You shouldn't be in this meeting. As your agent, I should be handling this."

"I'm sorry you feel this way, Lisa, but I want to play this out."

Lisa fumed and picked at the front of her pantsuit jacket, and stared at the blank tablecloth in front of her.

I was going to try to say something comforting to Lisa, when Nathan Barksdale appeared at the door to the room. Emily greeted him and shook his hand while Lisa sulked.

"Good morning all," boomed Barksdale. He moved between Lisa and me and shook our hands.

We all took our seats. Billie deposited pitchers of ice water and glasses on the table. We helped ourselves to water and Billie departed.

Barksdale said, "Well, Jack, I spoke with our board this morning. I'm prepared to respond to the terms you laid out last night."

I looked over at Emily and she was already looking at me, taking my measure.

Lisa asked, "Nathan, do you have anything in writing?"

"Yes, but I want to go over the details before I pass it out. Are you okay with that?"

Lisa said, "Once you give us your response, I would like to huddle with Jack before we continue any further."

Barksdale said, "Of course." He looked at each of us. "The board liked your scheme for paying advances on royalties at the delivery of a draft. The compensation level for each novel was acceptable. They agreed to the three non-genre books at the amount you asked. We're good with editing at our expense. You will approve the galleys. If we terminate your contract early, we will pay the termination fee you suggested. If you fail to perform, then we owe you nothing. The board was good with everything until we reached the stock and board seat.

"Reynolds and Ryan is a publically traded company, as you know. Substantive changes in financial position influence share prices. To give you stock, we would have to expand the number of shares of the company. This would dilute the percentage of ownership of each shareholder. While the board might be receptive to this, the shareholders wouldn't. Such an action would need shareholder approval. The board isn't in favor of bringing this up at an annual meeting.

"I huddled with our financial folks and we have an alternative. We will fund a retirement account. There will be three deposits made into this fund equal to one-percent of the value of the total shares of the company. We will make one deposit when you sign the first contract. When you've signed the first renewal in three years, we will make another deposit of one percent. In six years, with the second contract renewal, we will make the third. Once a year, we will adjust the amount in the fund to reflect any change in the value of the stock. It will be like a faux stock. Financially, it will be the same as owning it. This is the best I can do, Jack."

I asked, "What about the board seat?"

"They said no. Wall Street wouldn't favor a move like that. That's non-negotiable. I tried, Jack. It is just out of the question."

I was just about to respond to Barksdale, when Lisa spoke up. "Nathan, is that all?"

"No. If Jack accepts the more graduated faux stock arrangement, we will raise payment for each completed draft to one-point-three-million. The offer is good until tomorrow afternoon at five. I hope to leave town with a signed agreement." To me, Nathan said, "Jack, this is a significant offer. We've made a good team for many years. I hope we can continue to work together."

Lisa leaned over to me and said, "Don't say a word."

To Barksdale, Lisa said. "Let's take a ten minute break. I would like to talk with Jack and Emily for a few."

"Of course. I'll be at the bar."

When Barksdale left, Lisa said to me. "I would like you to leave the room and let Emily and me work with Nathan. Let us do our job. I think there is more on the table than he's offering."

"Alright, but having access to that board is important to me."

"Let me work on it."

Lisa stood and backed away from the table, my signal to leave.

It was nearing lunch. As I left the room, I roamed into Billie's office and asked if we could eat together. I wanted to talk with her about Alex's concerns. With Jody's mother arriving later today, I would have limited opportunity to talk with her. We found a table in the back corner of the courtyard and I observed Lisa and Barksdale sitting at the bar deep in discussion.

"Well, Monday is the night!" Billie combed through her short rusted red hair with her fingers.

I thought for a moment. "Oh, your lease burning party."

"It's my slowest night of the week. After the Conch Celebration ends on Sunday, things should be dead." Then she had this shocked, open mouth expression on her face. "Oh, crap! I forgot to tell Alex about the party. I was going to tell her yesterday, but she took off for Atlanta before I got the chance."

"She already knows. I talked with her before she left."

"Well, she won't be happy about that."

"Billie, that's what I wanted to talk to you about."

"Alex is mad because I forgot to tell her about the party?"

"No. It's more than that."

"What is it then?" She leaned in toward me and rested her folded hands on the tabletop.

"She said that since you received my father's inheritance, you've been distant. Independent was the word she used. She felt like you didn't need her anymore. I told her I didn't think that was true.

"And she felt like she couldn't talk to me?"

"I don't think she felt that she couldn't talk to you. She didn't want to make an issue if there wasn't one. So do you feel that way?"

"God, no."

"So what's going on?"

"This is so personal, Jack. Are you sure you want to wade into this?"

"I would prefer that you and Alex work this out and I wasn't in the middle. But if I can help, I want to."

Billie straightened up in her chair and rubbed her eyes. "Okay. Since Alex and I got together, I have wanted to have a baby. She hasn't been in favor of it because of the health risk at our ages. It has been the source of some difficult discussions between us. She wants to adopt, and I want to have a baby. Both options are expensive. Before your father put me in his will, we were so deep in debt the discussion was hypothetical. Now we have the resources to go either direction."

She reached across the table and grabbed my arm. "I want to have a baby, Jack."

"And what about the age concerns. You're what fifty-one?"

"Soon to be fifty-two. And that's the point." She squeezed my arm for emphasis. "There is still a chance for me through artificial insemination. Yes, there are risks involved. But every minute that passes the chances of failure increase."

"So you haven't talked with Alex about this?"

"In the past, when we've talked about it, we yell at each other, we don't talk. Alex's is afraid that something will happen to me."

"And you're not concerned?"

"I'm feeling more comfortable all the time. I've been seeing a fertility specialist in Miami. She feels my health is good enough to attempt it. They would impregnate me with a fertilized egg. It costs a fortune, but the doctor is optimistic. She assures me at the first sign of complications they could abort the fetus."

"What about childbirth? Do you feel you're up for that?"

"C-Section. That removes much of the risk."

"And when were you planning to share this with Alex?"

"My doctor wants to run a few more tests before she can recommend the procedure. I didn't want to tell Alex until I had all the loose ends tied up."

It was at moments like this when the full impact of Billie's homosexuality hit me. My own internal moral struggle with same sex relationships still simmered. When Billie presented me with her sexual orientation, I reasoned that she was my sister and I loved her. While I was not prepared to accept her homosexuality, I could and did accept her. Since then, I've set the moral issue aside. There had been too many people, including my mother and father who'd abandoned Billie over the issue. I didn't want to be one of them; I wouldn't be one of them.

She poured out her soul about this most basic human desire, having a baby.

"So when are you going to talk to Alex?"

"End of next week. That's when all the tests results will be available."

"I wouldn't wait that long, Billie. She's sick with worry, enough to ask me to intervene on her behalf. That took a lot for her to do that."

"You're right, Jack. I shouldn't have kept this from her. She should be home tomorrow night. I'll talk to her then. Maybe you should stay at Jody's, give us some room to hash this out."

At the mention of Jody's name, I thought about Helen Holland's impending arrival. I wondered how Jody was handling the stress of seeing her mother again. If I was anxious about it, Jody must be reeling with questions. When I left her this morning, she seemed to be coping. I wanted to catch up with her this afternoon and try to encourage her.

Twenty

Billie and I finished our lunch. She rushed off to meet her liquor distributor's truck to restock her supplies. I remained at the table with my thoughts. I looked over at the bar where Barksdale and Lisa had been sitting. Barksdale was gone, but Lisa walked toward me.

"Well, did you get all Barksdale's money?"

She sat down in a huff where Billie had been sitting. She pulled at the collar of her white blouse, then took a napkin from the table and blotted her forehead. She was miserable in a pantsuit, but her unwavering commitment to professionalism would rule.

"Not all, but more. I want to run some things by you and get your reaction."

"Alright."

"Let's talk about the board seat. Your concern was the board could make decisions about your future without your input. Right?"

"Yeah, I guess that's fair."

"Barksdale doesn't like the fact that you could go around him to his board. I have a solution. If you and Barksdale reach an impasse on an important issue, the board would arbitrate. You and Barksdale would both present your position to the board with both of you in attendance. Then the board would decide the issue. In addition, neither

Barksdale nor the board could fire you again until they heard your side. We would write this into your contract. Would that make you feel better? He won't like it, but I think I can get him to agree to it."

If I had been Barksdale, I wouldn't have liked my idea either. "Yeah, that would work."

"On the stock. I checked with our tax attorney at the agency. He liked R&R's retirement contribution scheme more than he liked you owning stock. If they gave you stock, the IRS would take a big hunk immediately. Under Barksdale's scheme, you will be able to defer the income taxes on a lot of it. Are you okay with it?"

"If I don't sign future contracts, I leave money on the table. That gives them a negotiating advantage when the contract renews. I don't care for that."

She said, "I know, that's why they want to do it. What if we ask for two percent on the first contract, and a half percent on contracts two and three?"

"Yes, I can live with that."

"So if I can get him to agree on these points, do you want to go with R&R?"

"Yes, it is a better package than the others. I like the fact that if my books improve the value of the company, I'll benefit. The other point is that I know R&R. I know their people. We've worked together and they get good results."

"Let me get back to work, then."

"Lisa, I appreciate your patience with me."

She nodded without speaking. Then she said, "Thank you for letting me do my job."

Lisa flitted off toward the bar, her cell phone to her ear, talking to Barksdale no doubt, wherever he was.

I called Helen Holland.

"Hi Helen."

"Hi, Jack. My plane arrives at nine-thirty tonight and I'm staying at the Hilton Resort."

"Can I pick you up at the airport?"

"I'm fine, Jack. I arranged for a car to pick me up."

"Good. The three of us will meet at my sister's restaurant for brunch. I'll meet you in front of the hotel at nine-thirty in the morning. It's just a short walk from there to Billie's restaurant."

"That's good, Jackie. Thank you for all you're doing."

Twenty-One

I called Emily. I could hear her cell phone ring as she neared my table. I closed my phone and offered her a chair.

"No, Jack, I won't be staying. Lisa will fill you in on the details, but it appears we have a deal. Now we iron out the fine print. Do you want me to stay and help her put a contract together?"

"Yes."

"Billie asked me to stay for the lease burning party, but I think I'm going to head back to Mt. Dora. You okay with that?"

"Yes, I was going to suggest it."

"All I want you to know right now, is that I'm very sorry, Jack."

"I know. We've a lot to talk about, but this isn't a good time."

She said, "I understand."

"Where's Barksdale?"

"He went to round up his attorneys. Billie needs the private room for a party this afternoon. In a few minutes, we will congregate at a conference room at the Pier House to work out contract language."

Lisa walked up and now stood beside Emily.

Lisa said, "I guess Emily told you we have a deal, pending contract details and language, of course."

"That's good news, Lisa."

Lisa said, "Barksdale still wants to meet with you one-on-one. After we all gather at the Pier House, he wants to buy you a drink."

"What could he want to talk about that we haven't already beat to death?"

Emily said, "I think before he signs this agreement, he wants to take your measure, Jack. Your depression caused them a significant financial setback. I think he's looking for assurances from you that you have it under control. While he feels this new contract gives him better protection, the company is betting on you."

"So what does he want, a psych evaluation?"

Lisa said, "I don't know, for now it sounds like he wants an honest discussion about your depression."

To both of them I said, "I guess with this much money at stake, if that will make him more comfortable, I'm okay with it."

Emily said, "I'll set it up. Pier House Bar at four-thirty, okay, Jack?"

"That's fine."

Lisa and Emily scurried off to do battle and my head swam with the challenges in front of me. At every turn, broken or strained relationships seemed to confront me. There was Billie and Alex, Jody and her mother, and the dysfunctional relationship I had with Barksdale. Then there was Emily.

Billie and Alex's problems were a hard discussion away from resolution. I had done my part. I set that issue aside.

On my relationship with Emily, Jody and I had something in common. I couldn't compare my anger over Emily's infidelity with Jody's angst toward her mother. But there were similarities. My bout with depression drove Emily away. Helen Holland's depression destroyed her family and her relationship with her daughter. Helen and I were both sick. In that state of mind and without intending to, we hurt those we loved. The damage we both caused was irreparable.

If I pushed my anger aside, Emily's behavior was a natural consequence of my illness. Without intending to, I hurt her, drove her away, destroyed our marriage and snuffed her love. Did I want this to happen? No. It was the consequence of my depression and not my will or wish. This is what I shared in common with Helen Holland.

And Emily still wanted to work with me. That she cared at all, after the way I treated her, was not lost on me. So where did that leave Emily and me?

I was angry that she cheated on me with Decker. She bruised my ego. That she chose Decker over me was hurtful. But the real problem was I needed to let Emily go. Despite my feelings for Jody and recognition that Emily and I would never get back together again, I was still hanging on to her. I had no idea why.

And there was Jody and her mother. The gulf between Emily and me seemed insignificant by comparison. I had no idea what Helen Holland expected in reuniting with Jody. From my vantage, any reconciliation beyond Jody's restrained toleration of her mother seemed impossible. The fact that Jody was even willing to meet her mother only hinted at the character of a woman for whom my respect grew daily. How would the meeting go? Nothing in Jody's actions or demeanor rendered a clue. The fact that she was nervous and concerned about how it would go, hinted at the meeting's importance. The whole idea of them getting together worried me. Jody had endured enough pain. A past filled with hurt for Jody was all I could envision from this meeting.

At four-thirty, I met Barksdale at the Chart Room Bar at the Pier House. Decorated in various shades of wood, embellished with nautical collectibles, maritime flags and model sailing ships, this storied local haunt grabbed me as soon as I walked in. I made mental note of the scene, wanting to remember it for some future novel.

Barksdale sat at a table flanked by a small bowl of peanuts and another of popcorn. Gone was his suit and in its place a short sleeved floral shirt and white Bermuda shorts. His fleshy arms and legs were pale white. He adorned his feet with flip-flops.

"Well Nate, this is a first, you without a suit."

He had a tumbler in front of him filled with what I assumed was Dewar's Scotch, his beverage of choice.

"When in Rome . . ." he said, held up his glass to me in a mock toast and then took a hit from his drink. "Sit, sit." He pushed a chair out on the opposite side of the table with his foot.

I circled the table then sat in the proffered bentwood chair. Barksdale signaled to the bartender. Without asking, two scotch-on-the-rocks appeared. I hated scotch, but I was not offended at the gesture. As long as I have known Nathan Barksdale, in his presence, I drank scotch.

"So, Nate, you wanted to talk about my depression?" I wanted to skip past the pleasantries.

"Geez, Jack. You're in a mood aren't you? It's been a long time since we had a drink together. What three or four years? Can't we just catch up a little?" Barksdale's pudgy face already had the pink glow of alcohol.

"Alright, Nate. What would you like to talk about?"

"First, I wanted you to know that I'm pleased that we were able to come to a deal."

"I am too, Nate." I meant it.

"But you're still pissed that I fired you?"

"What makes you say that?"

"When you're angry you call me, Nate. You know how I hate it when you call me that."

"You're right. I'm still angry."

"You have a right to be angry. At the same time you have to understand that you put us in a tight spot."

"I understand that. I didn't choose depression, Nate . . . Nathan. I was sick. It wasn't deliberate."

"I couldn't help the financial events that led to the board's decision, either. Your illness created problems that took on a life of their own. So, I'm not going to apologize for the company's actions. Any business, faced with those complications, would have done the same thing. That doesn't mean that I didn't fail. At the meeting, I only hinted at my culpability concerning your health issues. I saw the beginning signs of trouble and I did nothing. For that, I'm sorry. I confess that it was ignorance on my part about your depression. I saw your illness as a choice. You needed help and I failed you. If you will forgive me, I pledge that that won't happen again."

"I appreciate your contriteness, Nathan. I'm not sure that you or anyone could have done much, even if you were so inclined. It took a lot for you to ask my forgiveness and you have it without question. Emily and Lisa hammered me every day to get help and they were as close to me as anyone was. I was going to a counselor twice a week for much of that time and then I finally gave up. It wasn't until I considered suicide that it got my attention. As broken as I was, I knew unless something changed, I was a dead man. Until I reached that point, your help would have been a wasted effort."

Barksdale tossed the remains of his scotch back and signaled the bartender for another round. My glass was still full.

"Jack, I appreciate you letting me off the hook, but there are so many things I could have done and didn't."

I said, "You seemed to have experienced an epiphany, Nathan."

"My middle daughter. A month ago, I got a call from Mount Sinai Hospital that she'd over-dosed on sleeping pills. She has had continuing problems with depression, drugs and alcoholism. My lack of empathy and tough-love stance isolated her from me, and I almost lost her. We got her into counseling and I met with her doctors who told me she was suffering from bi-polar disorder. They assured me that choice had nothing to do with her condition. She needed medications and a better strategy for coping with stress. This all came on the heels of your situation with Reynolds and Ryan. I swore then, if I had the opportunity to make it right with you, I would."

Nathan's story touched me. "I'm so sorry, Nathan. How is your daughter doing?"

"Struggling. They haven't found the right combination of drugs yet. Her docs say she's still 'below the line', as they call it." He made quotation marks in the air with his fingers. "She's better, though. What have you learned from your experiences? Anything that might be helpful to, Janine?"

"Depression can be physiology or caused by bad thinking or both. In my case, I had built my self-esteem on the quicksand of my father's destructive criticism. I grew up with self-destructive attitudes, thanks to him. I had been replaying recordings of my father's harsh words as though I had merited them. In my depressed state, I thought and acted as though my father's words were true. Once I saw where the negativity was coming from, and began to ignore it, things improved. With some encouragement from someone who loved me, I was able to begin writing again. I was able to accept myself and I'm still learning to like the person I've become."

This was the first time, I had articulated to anyone my current mental state following my long illness.

"I have been an awful father, Jack." Barksdale fought hard to control his emotions.

My heart went out to him. "Nathan. Knowledge is power. What Janine needs from you is your love."

"I'm sorry to hear about your divorce, Jack. That had to be tough. I know how much you two loved one another."

"Still is tough."

"It sounds to me like you're on the other side of things. I would like to ask for your word on something."

"Alright."

"If you begin to struggle again, would you call me?"

"If it begins to affect my work, yes, I will."

"This isn't about work, Jack. This is personal. Will you reach out to me?"

"Yes."

We talked for another hour about the publishing business. I learned from him what was trending and shared with him projects that I had in mind for my next books. I had seen a side of Nathan Barksdale I hadn't seen before. Away from discussion of my health and his daughter, the bombastic, over-confident side of Nate reemerged. Our soul-to-soul conversation removed any doubts I had had about re-upping with R&R. I had connected with Barksdale at a level that made me comfortable about our future.

Twenty-Two

On the Havana Docks, Jody Holland looked across the table at Emily McNamara. At Jack's suggestion, Jody caught up with Emily at The Mangrove and suggested they talk. Jody knew Nathan Barksdale had Jack tied up in the Pier House Chart Room, so they agreed to meet after Emily finished with R&R's attorneys. Mallory Square, knotted with people, was Mecca to the Conchs who worshiped the sunset. If the island were a boat, it would capsize as the Conchs moved from one side of the island to the other, to drink, to party and to partake of the daily ritual at sunset.

Emily's attractiveness, intelligence, out-going confident personality and openness impressed Jody. They picked a spot far away from the live reggae music. Once they ordered margaritas, Emily broke the ice.

"Jack and I are sideways right now and I could use your help," Emily said.

"How?"

"I confessed to him yesterday that I had had an affair with his best friend while he was so sick. I told him that Bob and I are getting married soon. He was pretty upset."

"Yes, he was."

"What did he say to you about it?"

"That you 'betrayed' him. That was his word, not mine."

"Well that's fair, I guess. I feel terrible about it. After all that he has been through it was hard to drop that on him."

"What happened, Emily, if you don't mind me asking?"

"You mean, why did our marriage fail? Well, the depression Jack fell into was the crowning blow, but living with a writer was not easy, especially one as prolific as Jack. If Jack isn't writing, he's thinking about writing. When we went out to dinner, he has this far away glaze in his eyes and I knew his head was in the story he was writing. When he took a break, during the day, he may have been with me in body, but his head was off on some distant adventure. The problem was he was seldom with me. Distracted, and always in his head, the only way I got his attention was to walk into his studio naked. Even then, I wondered if I had his complete attention.

"And that was when things were good between us. Don't get me wrong, I loved him. I loved the work, his writing, the process of pulling a novel together and working with and for him. At the same time, the marriage part was hard. Then when he got sick and withdrew into that hole of his, I couldn't handle it. At first, I focused on trying to get help for him. I tried to find out what was wrong and tried to fix him. That was a disaster. He didn't want me fixing him and got angry when I tried. I finally gave up.

"I only had two people I felt comfortable talking with; Jack's father and Bob Decker, his best friend. Bob was just coming off a divorce of his own, so we commiserated. A bond developed and he began meeting needs of mine that Jack had no clue about."

"Are you saying that Jack is self-centered?"

"No, I would say self-contained. He needed me in many ways, but not emotionally."

"So why did you wait so long to tell him about Bob."

"When Jack became depressed, he fell apart. When I left him, he almost took his own life. If I had told him then about Decker, there is no telling what he would have done. It was wrong to deceive him, but it would have been worse had I told him."

"Why now?"

"He's stronger now, and I work for him, at least I did. I don't know what he's going to do. Bob and I are getting married soon. I had no choice. I had to say something."

"Why do you need my help?"

"I still care about him. I love to work for him. I love the work that we do and the books we create. He's an awesome boss. Work wise, he and I are compatible. Our relationship survived because of the work. The work alone was not enough. I needed more, and at the time, he was incapable of meeting those needs."

"So this is about your job?"

"Yes. I know him. I know what he wants, what he likes and what he doesn't. I know Reynolds and Ryan. Now that he's going to sign with them, I know all the players and have worked well with them over the last eight years."

"What do you want me to do?"

"Support me. Convince him that my staying is in his best interests, which is true. My message to you is that I'm not a threat. It is obvious that you love him. I don't want you to think that there is any possibility that we could be involved again. I'm in love with Bob Decker."

"What about him, Emily? Do you think he stills loves you?"

"Until yesterday, I would have said, yes. After I dropped the news about Bob on him, I would hope that that would have sealed the deal."

"He is still pretty angry. That tells me that there is something there."

Emily said, "One thing you need to understand about Jack. He's a loyal person, to a fault. He has friends that he has had since his childhood. He hangs on to people long after they've moved on to other relationships. I can understand why he's having a hard time letting go. Here's the thing, though. He'll be that way with you, if he isn't there already. What you're asking me is, 'Does he love me?' I can't answer that question."

"I appreciate your honesty, Emily."

"My friends call me, Em."

"Em, it is then."

Twenty-Three

"We need to talk. I don't think I can do this."

When I reached out to Jody by cell phone, these were the first words out of her mouth. She told me she was on the Havana Docks, that she and Emily had talked and that I should come and join her.

Barksdale had just left to meet with his attorneys and to get an update on the progress of our contract language. I finished my scotch, and wended my way out to the Havana Docks. The sun set in a cloudless sky to the oohs and aahs of an adoring audience. Jody sat alone on the far end of the deck. I bent over and kissed her then took my seat with my back to the remnants of the setting sun.

"I can't do it, Jack." I stretched across the table and took her hands in mine.

"Talk to me. What's going on?"

"It is too painful. The closer we get to her arrival, the more vivid the memories are of what happened. Those images of my brothers and sisters . . . well, they're a daylight nightmare." Her chin quivered as she held her emotions in check. "I just can't push those images out of my mind, and I'm so angry." She squeezed my hand to the point of pain.

"Don't meet with her," I said, despite the fact that her mother's flight had landed in Orlando, and she would soon leave for Key West. "It is just that simple. I'll call her and tell her that it won't work."

"I keep telling myself that I don't need this. I've made it this far in life without seeing her. Why am I doing this?"

"Jody, you don't have to see her."

"What will we achieve after all these years? What, Jack?" she asked rhetorically. "What does she expect from me? She tried to kill me. I just can't do it. I won't do it."

"Alright, I'll call her." I let go of her hands, stood up and pulled my cellphone out to call Helen and beg off.

"Hold it, Jack."

I sat back down and laid my cellphone on the table.

"I'm a mess right now. I hate her. I hate what she did to my family. What she did to me. But . . ."

Jody had been looking at the sun behind me, the crowds around us, her hands – everywhere but at me. Then she set her eyes on mine.

"She's my mother. I feel like the girl who woke up that morning after she shot me, with the bloody bodies of my family laying everywhere. I should have let her kill herself. I should have killed her myself for what she did, but I was as torn then as I am now. She's my mother. As much as I hated what she'd done to my family, I couldn't let her kill herself. When I wrestled the gun away from her, all those years ago, it was instinctual. Despite all my feelings to the contrary, I fought to save her life. What she did was horrible and I want to scream I'm so angry. But, she's my mother."

I had nothing to offer, except my silence.

"Jack, what should I do?"

I said nothing. I again reached across the table and took her hands in mine.

"You think I should meet with her, don't you?"

With eyes locked on one another, she conducted her own personal war within herself.

"She's on her way, isn't she?"

I continued to hold her hand.

"I need you to hold me," she said.

Without letting go of each other, we stood. With the crowd around us cheering the last vestiges of dying sun, she hugged me as a drowning swimmer might latch on to a lifeguard. The intensity of that embrace, reminded me of the last time I'd seen Jody as an adolescent. We were in the hospital after the shooting but before Jody's aunt came to take her to Atlanta. We knew that we wouldn't see one another again. We held each other with the same intensity then. The nurse had a difficult time separating us. When she finally succeeded, and as the nurse escorted me out of Jody's room, Jody said, "I'll never forget you." As I held her now, I acknowledged she'd made good on her commitment.

It was several long moments before she pulled away from me. "I couldn't go through this without you, Jack."

We stood there for a few moments holding hands as worshipers straggled off the deck with the disappearance of the last rays of the sun.

"What would you like me to do?"

"Don't cancel it," she said, without conviction. "I can get through it if you're with me."

We sat back down. Ordered margaritas, and stayed until the reggae band stopped playing. She didn't bring up her fears again, but it took a while before the darkness of the moment passed.

I paid the bar tab, and as we were descending the stairs from the Havana Docks, she said, "My talk with Emily didn't turn out anything like I'd expected."

"What did you talk about?"

"You. She asked me to lobby for her. She likes her job and wants to keep it. She thinks I can influence your decision."

"What did she say?" As we walked, the breeze off the water and the balmy temperatures were delightful.

"She said she still cares for you. She knows you're angry with her, but hopes you'll get over it and that you'll be able to work together."

"How do you feel about that?"

"Do you mean do I feel threatened by her?"

"Alright, let's begin there."

"No, I'm not worried about, Em. I'm not sure how I feel about having your ex-wife so close, but, no, I'm not threatened by her. It's you I'm concerned about."

"Why?"

"You went ballistic when she told you about marrying your best friend. That hit you hard. I guess I want to know if you still love her."

She was asking a question for which there were no definite answers. Despite the bomb Emily dropped on me concerning Bob Decker, I still cared for her. The deceit of my best friend doubled my anger.

Jody must have taken my hesitation as a negative. She stopped me on the sidewalk across from the Pier House. "Jack, I know you love me. If I had doubts about it, I wouldn't be here. Em, wants to continue to work for you. What concerns me is if you still have feelings for her, it will be difficult for you if she's still around."

"I have the same concern about Bob Decker and my continued relationship with him." Without answering her directly, I said, "A number of issues concern me about Emily working for me. I'm in love with you. If Emily interferes in any way with my relationship with you, then our professional relationship ends, it's just that simple. Yeah, I'm angry. Part of that hurt stems from my bruised ego and the realization that Bob Decker cut my legs out from under me. I have to work through that. You're more important to me than, Emily. Whether Emily stays is a decision I still have to work through. Right now, I'm still too angry to think about it. So, can we set this topic aside for a time?"

"I'm good, Jack. I know you'll make the right call."

"We'll make the right call."

Twenty-Four

I walked Jody home last night and then went back to Billie's. I had difficulty sleeping. I tried to write and to put a kernel of a story together based on Jody and her mother's experiences. I couldn't pull it together. I couldn't wrap my thinking around the enormity of the emotional damage done to Jody. I couldn't fathom how anyone could recover from such monstrous events and keep their mental balance. I tried to empathize with both of these women and I could not.

It was Saturday morning. Lisa Catera awakened me with a call.

"What's up, Lisa," I said, trying to reboot my mind from sleep.

"We burned and turned, Jack, and we finished the contract. I've run it past our agency attorneys and I've read and reread every word. Emily and Barksdale went through it last night and we all agree it is ready for you to sign. Barksdale took a flight out last night. He said he had family matters that needed his attention. He signed the contract before he left. It just needs your John Hancock, Jack. I stopped by Billie's house this morning and left the document there for you to sign."

"Nice job, Lisa. I appreciate all your hard work."

"I understand from Billie that personal things will tie you up this morning. If you will sign the contract and leave it on Billie's front porch, I'll pick it up and then head back to New York. Emily told me to tell you she's flying out with me. You might give her a call. She was an enormous help working out the details of the contract."

"Thanks again, Lisa."

I looked at my watch; it was after nine. In a panic, I called the Hilton, went through the switchboard and the operator connected me to Helen's room.

"I was beginning to worry a little, Jack. We're still on?"

I told her I would meet her outside the front door in an hour and then we would walk to the restaurant. I called Billie and Jody and set a time to meet. Billie assured me that she had everything under control. She warned me about taking Duval Street. She said The Conch Republic Independence Celebration had the streets clogged and that I should come the back way.

I called Emily.

"I'm going to leave with Lisa," she said, "I'll leave the keys to your SUV at the front desk at the Pier House."

"Thank you, Emily. You've been a big help. When is the wedding?"

"Next weekend."

"We'll talk before then."

"Jody is marvelous. I think we can be good friends. She told me about her mother coming today. I'm praying that it will go well."

"Thanks again, Em."

After I showered and dressed, I bounded down the stairs to the kitchen. I couldn't find Mrs. Berger, but a manila envelope addressed to me in Lisa's scrawl sat on the kitchen counter. I scanned the legal gobbledygook, and homed in on the specific terms. It was as perfect as I'd expected. I signed my name, shoved the papers back in the envelope and walked out the front door. I propped the sealed envelope up on a porch chair for Lisa to pick up. I thought about Nathan Barksdale's daughter and hoped that better days lay ahead. I made a mental note to call him in a week or so for an update.

I recognized Helen Holland at once. She was just shy of five feet and paced back and forth under the Hilton's porte cochère. She wore a long pink sleeveless dress that hung to her feet, accented with a single strand of pearls. Her hair was jet black, cut short in the style of a man. Other than the pearls, she wore no jewelry and no make-up. Her bowed posture hinted at Osteoporosis and her gaunt face and sunken eyes made her appear older than her seventy-three years. As I approached, her smile was warm and she seemed happy to see me.

I met her outstretched arms, bent over and hugged her. She felt as bird frail as she appeared.

"Jackie. Look at you," she said, pulling away from me. "As handsome as ever."

"You look wonderful as well."

"You're lying, Jackie, but I won't hold it against you. As they say, I've been ridden hard and put up wet."

I chuckled at her self-deprecation. "Are you good with a short walk?"

"Yes, yes," she said with vigor. What an enchanting place. I took a stroll early this morning. It is Charleston, and New Orleans rolled into one place."

I'd never heard Key West described so true. "A little bawdy and a little refined. And a whole lot of history," I said.

"Yes, exactly. What an interesting setting for a novel, and you're a Hemingway fan, are you not? I thought about you as I walked past his old home."

"Yes, I love it here. The place oozes with character."

"And, Jody? Does she like it here?"

I told her about Jody's art gallery and her success with featured local artists.

"And, she's happy?"

"Yes, happy describes it."

"So, Jack, what am I walking into this morning?"

"I'm not sure I know what you mean." I thought her question was odd.

"What is my daughter's state of mind?"

"I don't want to try to answer that, Helen. You wanted the opportunity to meet with her. She was willing to do it. Given the circumstances, I would be thrilled at the opportunity."

"Oh, Jackie, I am. Don't misunderstand. I was just trying to gauge how big a mountain I have to climb."

"That's something you should judge for yourself."

We engaged in pleasantries the rest of the way to The Mangrove. There were several times along our path that I marveled at how petite Helen was. If I didn't know the history, it would be hard to convince me that someone of her diminutive stature could have caused such carnage.

When we appeared at the doorway to the private dining room, Jody sat with her hands folded on the table. She stood and said nothing. I tried to read her, but her face was expressionless.

Helen said, "Jody, dear."

We approached the single, round table in the middle of the room. Billie had garnished the table with flowers, and set coffee, water and orange juice out in appropriate decanters. Sweet rolls overlapped each other on a plain white dish. Cups, saucers, glassware and settings for three marked our places at the table. We all sat.

Jody looked at me, then at her mother. She swallowed hard and said, "Mother, I have no idea where to begin."

Helen said, "Yes, well, I've thought about this moment for years. Now that it's here, it's hard to know where to start except to say how sorry I am for what happened."

Jody furrowed her brow, narrowed her eyes and asked, "Why did you do it? All these years, all I ever wanted to know was, why?"

"I was sick. I saw my family sliding into Hell and I was powerless to stop it. The threat of Hell was so real to my delusional mind, I felt I had no choice but to do what I did. I wanted my family to be in heaven with God. I thought I was such a bad mother, that I couldn't keep my children from harm, and that the only way to save them was to take them to Heaven with me. That was the only place they would be safe. That was my reality. I wanted to protect my family, and ending our lives was the only way to do it."

Jody asked, "In the statement you gave to the police, you said, "The children had no mother or father."

Helen answered, "In the state of mind I was in, I believed your father and I had become corrupt. Your father and I were no longer able to care for you or your brothers and sisters. We could no longer protect you from the hell we were sliding into. This Hell was so real, so horrifying, I didn't feel that we could go on anymore. I had to do something – I had to rescue my family. I believed I had no choice.

"Of course none of it was real, but at the time, in the state of mind I was in, it was all too real and horrifying. I felt dead inside, like a walking corpse. It horrified me that you were sliding away to the same place I was. I knew what I was doing was wrong, but, at the same time, I knew that I didn't have a choice.

"And this is the part of mental illness that people don't understand – what we believe and think is our reality." She emphasized the word 'is.' "We act based on what we believe this reality to be. When a person is delusional, it is as real to them as anything in a normal person's life. These delusional states are horrifying realities. In these states, the mentally ill suffer beyond anything a mentally healthy person can imagine. So I go back to my short answer, I did it to protect my family."

Jody asked, "How do you live with what you did?"

"Jody, I have no choice. I can't go back and change what happened. I can choose to live, or I can choose to take my own life as so many PPP women who've committed infanticide have done. Even with counseling and outside help, these poor souls cannot live with the consequences of their actions. With counseling and support from other PPP women, they can survive. The problem is that the people around them, their families and friends, the communities they live in cannot accept what they did. This rejection by most everyone in her world is the greatest obstacle to a PPP survivor's recovery.

"When I had Robert, I was mentally ill. The psychosis and the departure from reality made me into someone different. I became a victim of the disease and the disease turned me into someone else. The person who took the lives of my children and husband was not me. I was physically and mentally sick. While it was me physically, it was not me mentally. You were not the only victim, Jody. You, your dad, and your brothers and sisters were not the only victims. I was a victim of this awful disease, too.

"Before I had a chance of getting mentally healthy again, I had to understand that it was not me who took the lives of my family. It was not my fault. I was not in my right mind, and I couldn't hold myself responsible for what happened. It was hard for me to see this until another woman came to South Florida State Hospital who'd also taken the life of her baby. When I saw this poor woman, and listened to her story and the horror she went through during her psychosis, it was only then that I realized that this woman was not herself when she took the life of her baby. She was a victim of this horrible disease. What I couldn't see in myself, I could see in this woman. She'd suffered severe trauma during childbirth and had morphed into this paranoid, depressed and psychotic woman. It was plain to me that she was not a murderer. She loved her baby. In her warped and delusional state, she took her baby's life out of fear that her baby was in danger. It was apparent, that it was not the woman's fault, that she was the victim not the perpetrator.

"It was then that I recognized that the healthy me, the real me, didn't commit these acts. That I had no chance of survival, I had no life ahead of me, if I couldn't accept that truth. I had to forgive myself for what the physical me had done."

"It was 1966, six years after they admitted me to the hospital before I grasped that important truth. That was the beginning, but I was a long way from being healthy again. Then, I couldn't distinguish between the mentally sick person

I was and the real, healthy, me. Emotionally, I still blamed myself for what happened, and I suppose that, to some extent, I'll always shoulder that blame. But, with the help of Dr. Carnes, I was able to put some distance between the healthy me and the sick person who took the lives of my family. I was able to box off that person, to isolate that incident, to forgive myself for something that was not my fault. That's when I began to make progress. In 1969, I walled off what happened, and I was able to put some emotional distance between it and me in a healthy state."

Jody began to ask a question, Helen held up her hand.

"And if you'll give me a moment more, when they released me from the hospital, I knew that I couldn't go back to my old life. I knew that while I might be able to forgive myself, I knew that my family and friends and the community would not. I had to disconnect myself from the old me. I had to start new. When I finished medical school, and internship, Dr. Carnes asked me to come back to South Florida and work with her. I tried for a short time, but I couldn't do it. It was too close, and I knew that I couldn't stay in Hollywood. I wouldn't succeed in picking up the pieces of my broken life there. So I moved to Tampa. Only then was I finally able to disconnect myself from the horrors of what happened in 1961. The separation between me and the person who took so many lives was almost complete."

Jody asked, "Where's the justice? Everything you've said is wonderful for you, but what about little Robert? What about Michael, Jeannie, Daniele and Dad? What about them? What about the lives that they could have led? Who speaks for them? This isn't just about you. What about me? What about the damage inflicted on me? I lost my whole family. I lost my childhood. How could you ever expect me to forgive you for what you did?"

There was a long silence as Helen and Jody looked hard at each other.

Helen said, "I'm not here to ask for your forgiveness. I didn't come here seeking it. We were all victims of a tragedy. You and I are both victims. But, before you respond, I want to address your question about justice. Last year in Kobe, Japan, a six-point-nine earthquake took the lives of more than five-thousand people. Where's the justice for them? Hurricane Andrew killed fifty-three people just three years ago, just a couple of hours north of here. Cancer takes the lives of countless thousands in the U.S. every year. Where's the justice for them? AIDS has taken countless lives in the last ten years. Who's at fault? Who'll take the blame? There will never be recompense for these tragedies. No one was at fault. These tragedies just happened.

"No one can measure the pain I have suffered over the years because of what I physically did to my family. Only God knows how much I have suffered because of it. I'm certain that for some, the only way I could pay for what I did would be to be put to death. If I believed I was in my right mind when I did what I did, then I would deserve to die. But I wasn't. I was sick. The justification for my life is that I can help prevent this from happening to other unsuspecting women. I can teach doctors and clinicians how to prevent this from happening to others. I have more value working to help others than I would if I took the easy way and ended my life."

Jody asked, "Then why did you want to see me if not to ask for my forgiveness?"

"I work with women and families who have to deal with consequences of infanticide. It still amazes me the extent of the emotional damage and the number of people this disease affects. While the fallout from infanticide extends well beyond the immediate family, it is the spouses and surviving family members, who suffer the most. I work with the victims ravished by this disorder. For the first twenty years, I focused on the mothers–helping them cope with the tragedy. Several years ago, I began to focus on the destruction that infanticide caused within the mother's immediate family.

"Husbands were so bitter and poisoned by what happened. Siblings, who couldn't get past the horror of what happened, saw their sisters as monsters. And, in our case, a surviving child so traumatized by what happened you had difficulty carrying on with your life. I noticed that the key to the recovery of all the damaged family members was letting go of what happened, to forgive and not to cast blame."

Jody said, "That sounds pretty self-serving to me. You want me to forgive you, so that "I" can heal. Sounds like you're looking for a free pass on what happened?"

"I know it sounds illogical, but you need to forgive me for yourself, not for me. This is why I wanted to see you. Yes, I admit that I wanted to be with you, my beautiful daughter. And yes, my wish and my prayer for many years is that one day we might be mother and daughter again. I admit that. But, I wanted to see you to explain that you will never heal from what happened until you let it go. You will not be able to let it go until you forgive. These negative emotions are a prison that will rob you of the pleasure of living. I have seen so many cases over the years where the inability to let the tragedy go has resulted in a mental illness all its own. It sucks the life out of its victims and brings them to their knees."

Jody said, "It already has." She paused as if searching for words on the backs of her hands folded in front of her. "I almost destroyed my life and spent a year in counseling. You're asking me to do something I'm incapable of doing. I would have to erase the faces of my dead brothers and sisters from my memory to do that. Their loss haunts me like a debt I need to pay, a failure I cannot escape. How can I forgive you, when I cannot forgive myself for letting it happen?"

"And so we've come to the point of my being here. None of this was your fault. You were a victim of something outside of your control. You cannot hold yourself responsible for what happened."

Jody said, "Just like you."

"Yes, just like me. I had no control over what happened. I was sick, a victim."

Then there was silence. A long silence. Jody sat, looking at her hands, then at me, but not at Helen. Helen gazed at Jody with the concern of a mother. She looked as though her heart were breaking for her daughter; the furrows in her brow, the way her eyes moved from Jody's feet up to her downcast face. She looked like she wanted to reach out and hug her. Silence fell upon us.

After a while Helen said, "I'm staying at the Hilton Resort for a few days. We should talk again after you've had a chance to digest what I've said."

Jody nodded. Her face was devoid of expression.

"Well, I should go." Helen stood.

Jody said, "Jack, you should walk her back to the hotel."

Helen said, "That's not necessary, Jack. I'll be fine."

Jody said, "Jack, I need some time to myself. I would feel better if you made sure Helen is comfortable."

Twenty-Five

Helen and I followed Duval Street toward the Pier House and talked as we walked. Tourists clogged the sidewalk.

"You're in love with her, aren't you? Helen asked.

"It's that obvious?"

"There is good chemistry there. I can see it in the way that she looks at you. She respects you; values your opinion."

"You want my help, don't you?"

"Now it's me who is obvious. Jack, you don't go through what Jody went through without significant emotional damage. Even though I can separate myself from what happened, I cannot separate myself from loving my daughter. What happened to her was the worst trauma you can imagine."

"What kind of damage?" I had been asking myself this question ever since Jody and I reconnected. She said that she'd been through counseling, but can anyone ever get over something so painful?

"I've had three patients who committed infanticide where there were no surviving children. I have never come across a case like ours where a psychotic mother tried to take the lives of all of her children and one of the children survived. Jody encountered the perfect storm of rejection. And it happened at a crucial time in her emotional development. Think about it, Jack. Her own mother tried to kill her. I can explain all day why it happened. But, down in her emotional wiring, there is a hurt so deep that nothing I can say will change it. Add to that the carnage of her beloved family in front of her. The stress I placed her under, and what she witnessed, one can only speculate on the damage done."

It was difficult carrying on a conversation. People pushed between us or we had to navigate around window-shoppers. There was a small courtyard next to an ice cream shop with tables and chairs for patrons. We sat in the shade at an empty table.

I continued, "Why forgiveness? If the damage done is as you describe it, how does forgiveness undo it?"

"It doesn't undo anything. Nothing can change what happened. What she has internalized from those events causes the emotional damage. The fact that she blames herself for not stopping me from taking the lives of her brothers and sisters is an issue I hadn't anticipated."

"I still don't understand, Helen."

"Negative emotions, like anger and bitterness toward others, when harbored and internalized are destructive. They eat away at our psyche like a cancer. Over a long enough period, they can control our thoughts and behavior. When we refuse to let go of these negative emotions, they can destroy us. They interfere with close intimate relationships and inhibit our enjoyment of life. They eat away at who we are.

"Forgiveness is a way to release these negative emotions, to get them out of us. In Jody's case, it will take counseling to dig up these negative feelings about her, and about me, and then let them go. Forgiveness is the key to doing that."

"She has already been through a lot of counseling."

"Do you think she has gotten over what happened to her?"

"No. I don't."

"That's why I'm here. I'm the focal point of her anger. She needs to confront it, with me."

"And how would she do that? It doesn't seem like you accomplished that this morning."

"It would take hours of joint therapy; perhaps two sessions a week."

"How do you see that happening? You live in Tampa. She lives here."

"I would move here for a short time."

"What about your institute?"

"I'm semi-retired now. There is nothing in my life more important than Jody's health."

"So assuming you both agree to counseling is there anyone here in Key West qualified to deal with these enormous issues?"

"No one I know. That's why I reached out to Dr. Carnes whom you and Jody met in Hollywood. She retires soon and has agreed to fly down, from Miami, as often as we need her."

"Won't flying Carnes in once or twice a week be expensive?"

"I have the resources to take care of it."

"Wow. That's a lot to throw on Jody at one time. I can assure you she has no inkling what you have in mind."

"That's why I don't plan on 'throwing anything on her,' as you say. I'm willing to go as fast or as slow as she wants to go." She paused then asked, "Do you think any of it got through? You know her better than I do."

"I was thinking while you were talking with Jody, that I have never encountered emotional issues so difficult to understand. I feel for both of you. If what you say is right, and this disease is transitory, I can't imagine what you've been through. One morning you wake up in a healthy state of mind and realize what you've done. What an impossible situation. And Jody, having to live her life with those kinds of emotional issues is incomprehensible. I can't see how she can function, yet she does, and she's a remarkable woman despite it all. I don't see how either one of you could get past it."

"And yet we must. We've no choice. We figure it out or it defeats us."

"I wish I could offer some suggestions, anything to help. But I can't. This is well beyond my experience."

"Come, let's walk some. My sciatic is killing me."

We got up, found a side street over to Whitehead and aimed for the Hilton.

"Do you blame me for what happened?"

"Helen, I can't answer that. I'm still processing what you said today. I guess I can say with some assurance that what happened to the Holland family was tragic. And from what I know of you, I don't believe, had you been in your right mind, you would have done what you did." I hesitated in saying what was on my mind.

"Say it, Jack. Don't hold back on me."

"I also feel that anyone who takes the life of another cannot be in a right mental state. Look at mentally disturbed serial killers, for example. They're on death row, or they're serving life sentences. What makes them different? Why can't they say that they were not in their right mind when they committed their crimes?"

"This is a valid point, Jack. I have asked myself this question, too. I admit that the answer I came up with for me may not satisfy you. Let me try.

"In the case of PPP, the mental defect relates to biological changes in the mother as a direct result of childbirth. The dramatic and temporary shifts in body chemistry create a psychotic state. This happens to a small percentage of women. The symptoms fade in a short time and then these women return to a healthy state of mind.

"Jack, PPP, stands alone as a unique and completely treatable mental phenomenon. Those PPP women experience great suffering. The phenomenon is so unique among mental illnesses I have no problem separating it from other violent psychotic homicides. "

"This is a lot to process."

"Indeed it is, Jack. And it is only the beginning."

"When do you want to get together with Jody again?"

"That's up to Jody. This is something she has to want."

"How long are you willing to wait?"

"Until you or Jody tell me to leave."

"Why now? Why is this so important after all these years?"

"My reasons are personal. I'll tell you this. While I may not be able to change the past, I do have one opportunity and only one opportunity, to make it right with Jody. I hope she'll give me that chance."

"You're asking a lot, Helen."

She reached for my hand. "I would give everything I have for my daughter's acceptance and understanding." She released my hand. "Now give me a hug and go find, Jody. After our time together, she'll need to talk to someone."

I bent over and hugged her. With her stooped posture, she turned from me, padded through the front door of the hotel and disappeared into the lobby.

Twenty-Six

I don't know what I expected would happen when Jody's mother came to talk with Jody? The romantic me conjured images of an intense scene, a breakthrough of some kind and mother and daughter ending the session in an embrace. The realistic me envisioned the breadth and height of the issues that separated them. That I didn't anticipate the long process to untangle the emotional knot that bound them shook my confidence. I had hoped I could be of meaningful help, but I knew then that was impossible. As I left Helen Holland at the Hilton, a feeling of helplessness overwhelmed me. I knew when I found Jody, she would want to talk about their meeting and ask for my opinion. She would want to know what Helen and I talked about. I couldn't withhold the prescription Helen suggested to reconstruct their estranged relationship. I knew there would be a storm of emotion attached to their reunion, but I didn't anticipate a hurricane. While I may have had a hint at the enormity of the issues, I was naïve about the monumental nature of the solution.

I called Jody and she was still at the restaurant. I decided to walk to Billie's via Duval Street. While this route was longer than the back way past Hemingway's house, I wanted to chew on the mornings events. I had forgotten that the Conch Republic Independence Celebration was in full-tilt. The police had Duval Street blocked to traffic. Halfway up Duval, at Fleming Street, beds on wheels of every conceivable description clogged the intersection.

Contestants cued up for the Conch Republic Bed Race, to benefit AIDS research. They would race down Duval, in heats of two, to the finish line at Petronia Street, a block or so from The Mangrove. At the starting line, two five-person teams, with one person occupying the "bed" readied for the start signal. On one team, men dressed in sexy nurse's costumes readied to push a patient in a hospital bed. On the second team, three women and one man, attired in hot pink bikinis, set themselves to propel a sports-car appearing bed with a passenger. Cheers and air horns sounded as the two teams bolted from the starting line. A wave of cheers and whistles followed them down Duval Street on their quest for bragging rights. Behind them, waiting for their turn, were men dressed as women, women dressed like men, men dressed like superheroes, ballerinas and even babies in diapers. As each team raced the distance, I could hear the hullabaloo all the way to Billie's restaurant. The sidewalk was almost impassable and it took fifteen minutes to walk the short distance up Duval.

The restaurant was full. It was hard to distinguish the line of people waiting to be seated from the revelers knotting the street. Patrons stood three or four deep at the bar waiting for service. I had to apologize my way through the throng at the bar to get to Billie and Jody. I tapped them on the shoulder. How they could talk in the din was miraculous.

Billie looked relieved to see me. I surmised that her staff needed her as they tried to cope with the army who'd placed her restaurant under siege. Billie's compassion for Jody kept her from her duties. She hugged Jody, patted me on the shoulder and headed off to the main building. I looked for somewhere we could retreat to, but patrons filled every seat. Just as we were about to give up and leave, Billie appeared. She and a server carried two wrought iron chairs and a small table to an empty spot in the shade at the rear of the courtyard. We sat and our server took our drink orders."

We both took a deep breath and let it out at the same time.

I said, "I've never seen it this busy."

"It's like this every time there is a big event. What a madhouse!"

It was warm in the courtyard, and only a wisp of a breeze caught the leaves of the Banyan tree above us. Jody had her hair pulled up into a ponytail, and beads of sweat formed on her forehead.

"Well don't keep me in suspense, tell me what she said."

"I'll be honest, Jody. I don't know where to begin."

"That's where I am. Overwhelmed."

I said, "Let's begin with you. What's your reaction? You looked upset while she was talking."

"She said the same thing Dr. Carnes told us. She was sick, she wasn't herself and it wasn't her fault. She was a victim just like the rest of us. And that upset me." Jody gave the word "that," a punch. "My reaction? Rage. That's the only word I can think of to describe what I was feeling while she talked. I had to fight hard to contain it."

I asked, "Do you believe her self-characterization as victim?"

"When I was talking to Billie before you came, I told her that it all boiled down to whether I bought into that argument." She ticked off the points again. "And I can boil it down to just one question, 'Was she sick?' And if I don't believe she was sick, the only other choice is that she did it with intention." She removed the umbrella from her drink, licked some of the salt off the rim and took a sip.

"You said you felt rage when your mom was talking."

"Anger, resentment, bitterness . . . wanting to tear her apart for what she did."

"Even after all this time?"

"Yes."

"What about the counseling that you went through? Didn't that help?"

"Some, yes. It made me see how self-destructive I was when I was younger. After counseling, I'm able to live with it. But, my mother is right. Although I've buried it and shoved it down, the anger eats at me, Jack. If I think about what happened to my family it is hard to contain. Seeing her, being in the same room with her dredges it to the surface. Now, would you please tell me what she said?"

"Her concern for you is genuine. She wants to help. In her opinion, you would both need to go through counseling together, for an extended period."

Jody nodded without comment.

"If you're willing, she wants to move to Key West, for a while. She said Dr. Carnes, the doctor we met at South Florida Hospital, has offered to help and will fly to Key West as often as needed."

"What are your thoughts, Jack?"

"I think her desire to help is sincere. She said she's willing to pay the cost of everything."

"I hate her, Jack, with every fiber in me. She has no idea what she's asking?"

"Then what do you want to do?"

"What do I want? I want to be free of it, Jack. I need to forgive her and I can't. I want to be free of my brothers and sisters calling out to me in nightmares. I want a future with you without bitterness nibbling at the edges of our relationship. Down where it counts, I worry that you don't want me, that you couldn't possibly love me. What happened to me—what my mother did—figures into all this. Because I hate her so, I know that I need help. I hate that she's right. I hate that tying me to her is the solution. But nothing I have tried has worked."

"Then you want to go through with this?"

"No, but do I have a choice?"

"So, have you answered the question whether you believe her? Was she sick?"

"You first."

"Alright. As someone who has suffered with severe depression, who almost took his own life, I understand I was not in my right mind. It was not the healthy me who went for the gun in my glovebox. At that moment, I felt like I had no choice. And if I hadn't been stopped by the Sheriff's deputy, I probably would have pulled the trigger. I was in a bad place.

"Nothing I experienced compares to what your mother went through. But, I believe her thinking could have been so corrupted and her reality so altered that she could have taken a life thinking she had no choice. From everything we've seen, from the police reports, to Dr. Carnes' explanation, to what your mother said and from what I know about her, I don't think we can hold her responsible for what happened. If anyone is to blame, it was your father, who could have prevented this if he'd followed the doctor's recommendation and left her in the hospital. Now, you."

"I feel like I have to betray my dad and my brothers and sisters. To agree with you, I must let my family go, each one of them, to forget what happened to them. As long as I hold on to the memory of them, they still live. To let my mom off the hook, I have to let them go. You've no idea, how difficult that would be."

"So you want to pursue this, then?"

"Yes."

"Do you want me to tell her?"

"We . . . we will tell her."

"When do you want to do this?"

"Now. This is my fifth margarita." She lifted her empty glass. "If I don't have the courage to do it now, I never will."

I called ahead and Helen suggested we meet in the hotel bar. By the time we got to the Hilton, Helen had already found a table and awaited our arrival.

Helen stood as we approached the table. I followed Jody's lead. I didn't try to hug Helen because I did not want to put Jody in the position of having to follow suit. Jody sat opposite from her mother and I sat next to Jody.

Jody got straight to it. "Jack told me you suggested that you and I go through counseling together."

"I wish there were another way," Helen said. "I don't know what Jackie told you, but this is going to take a while, a year or more. Are you sure this is something you want to do?"

"Yes, but I want you to know that I'm doing this for me, not for you."

"As well you should."

215

"And I make no commitments beyond giving it a try. I make no commitments to you. We do it as long as it makes sense. When it stops making sense, we stop."

"I think that's wise."

Jody looked over at me, then at Helen and said, "How do you want to do this?"

"Well, I suppose I need to find a place to rent for a while. Then I need to return to Tampa for my things. When I'm back and settled, I'll call you and we'll get started."

Jody reached into her purse, found a business card and slid it on the table to Helen. "Here's my cellphone number." Jody stood. Then Helen and I stood.

Helen said, "I know this is a small step, Jody. But this is an answer to a lifetime of prayer for me."

Jody said nothing.

Helen said. "When I have things set up, I'll call."

Jody said, "Good." With that, Jody got up from the table and walked out of the bar.

I looked at Helen, and caught a sense of relief on her face.

"Thank you," she mouthed the words.

I nodded, turned and followed Jody.

Once outside, Jody turned to me, broke into tears and said, "I have to let my family go, Jack. I'm drowning under the burden I'm carrying for them."

"Let them go, then. I'm sure if they were here they wouldn't want you carrying the weight of their lost lives on your shoulders. "

"I feel like I'm turning my back on them."

"You may feel that way, but is it true?"

"No." She wiped the tears from her eyes. "No, that isn't true." I could see in the way she looked at me that she'd set the burden aside. "Destroying myself, won't bring them back, will it, Jack?"

We weren't at Jody's house more than ten minutes before she was sound asleep on the couch. The combination of the alcohol and the stress of facing her past left her exhausted. Something happened to Jody, though, standing under the porte cochère at the Hilton, after we met with her mother. I could see it in her eyes. What I saw was hope.

It was early evening. As Jody snored, her head propped up on her hand; all I could think about was Emily. I had my own anger issues to deal with. What was I holding onto? What did I need to let go?

What was holding me? Was I still in love with Emily? Emily's tryst with Decker certainly extinguished any flame that remained. Was I angry with Emily for leaving me? No. I understood it. Was I angry with Decker? Yes, in a masculine turf-war kind of way. It bruised my ego. Was I willing to end my friendship with him over it? No. As I considered these emotional issues alongside of Jody and her mother's, they seemed petty. Did I want Emily back? No. Why would I want someone who didn't want me? The fact that she chose Bob over me was hurtful. Did it matter that much now? No. Did it mean that I couldn't work with her? No. Could I let go of her infidelity? Could I let go of her impending marriage to Bob Decker? Yes.

I walked out on Jody's front porch and called Emily.

"Jack, I just walked in the door. Everything okay?"

"That's why I'm calling, Em. Everything is okay." The emphasized the word 'is.'

"You mean the wedding, the job . . . what?

"Everything. We're good. I wish you and Bob the best."

"Oh, Jack. That's wonderful. I'm so sorry for the way it turned out."

"We're good, Em."

"Since we signed the contract and we don't have a book going, I thought I would take a few weeks off. Are you alright with that?"

"That's perfect. I want to do the same. When you get back from your honeymoon, let's touch base."

I flipped my cell phone closed, stood on the porch and considered my next moves. Light from the streetlight filtered through the trees and left dappled shadows on the front yard and porch. A breeze rustled the trees and I relished this moment. It was the first time in months, perhaps even years, I felt at peace with myself and at peace with those around me. My parents had fashioned the foundation of my life with flawed material. That underpinning crumbled under the weight of the storm forces of my life. I rebuilt them with stronger, more durable materials. It was still a work in progress, but from where I stood, poised to enter a new phase of my life, I was optimistic about the future.

I thought about my beloved Mt. Dora and the home and studio I had called home for a long time. I was not looking forward to my return. Bad memories abounded. From my current vantage, Key West felt more like home with each passing day. It was here that I had written my first words after a two-year case of writer's block. My only sibling was here, someone I loved and cared about. Jody was here and it seemed natural for me to be here as well. The fact was I loved Key West.

Twenty-Seven

Jody and I approached the host station at The Mangrove. A sign read. "Sorry, closed. PRIVATE PARTY." The deserted streets demonstrated the sign was not necessary. The Conch Republic Independence Day celebration had ended. The island's inhabitants had sighed in collective relief. Monday's dead quiet replaced yesterday's raucous, party atmosphere. We let ourselves through the gate and spied a small knot of people who'd gathered at the bar. They talked in moderate tones. The staff had set up serve-yourself hors d'oeuvre stations near the bar. Billie flitted between clusters of friends, welcoming them and seeing to their needs.

I recognized Mrs. Berger sans uniform and she actually smiled at me. Billie saw Jody and me standing alone together, and invited us to join her. She was standing next to Cynthia Pike, her attorney. Pike had dressed in a suit and looked like she'd come straight from the office. Billie introduced Jody, and Pike and I exchanged greetings. More than fifty people milled about, none of whom I knew.

"Jackie, could I speak with you for a moment." Billie pulled me away, leaving Jody to visit with Pike alone. "Alex and I had a major blow up last night. I knew it would happen. She got home from Atlanta yesterday and I told her about my visits to the fertility doctor."

"Well, what happened?"

"She was angry. But it wasn't about the baby. What upset her was I had kept all this from her. She said that I didn't trust her enough to tell her about it. That I would talk to you and not her. She was so angry I thought she was going to leave me."

"Well . . . don't leave me hanging here," I said.

"When she got up this morning she said she was over it. I promised her I wouldn't keep something like that from her again."

"Well, what about the baby? What did you decide?"

"Alex worries about my health, but she'll go with me to my next appointment. She said as long as the doctor felt I was not at risk, she was good."

"Are you excited?" I said.

"I am, Jackie. I am. There are a lot of bridges to cross before we get there and I don't want to get my hopes up."

Alex and Jody appeared.

"Get your hopes up about what?" Alex asked.

Billie said to all of us, "Alex and I are exploring the possibility of having a baby."

I looked at Alex and Billie and they both looked ecstatic, Alex more jubilant than I expected. She beamed.

"Well, I have an announcement of my own," I said. I looked at Jody and took her hand in mine. "I've decided to move to Key West."

Jody, Billie and Alex all congratulated me and expressed their happiness with my decision.

Billie tapped a goblet with a fork several times to get everyone's attention.

"I'm so pleased you all could make it tonight. I have been so fortunate. The restaurant has been such a success and I just wanted to celebrate it with the people who've been such a big part of it." Billie mentioned everyone pointing out each person's contribution in making The Mangrove a hit. "And most of all I want to thank, Alex. When I didn't have a penny to my name, she believed in me and invested every dime she had into this old run down restaurant. And when we ran out of her money, we borrowed more – actually she borrowed more. Thanks to my brother, his father and help from Cynthia Pike, I was able to buy the property, pay off our debts and invest in much needed improvements. But, it has been Alex who stood by me when no one else would. Alex risked it all, so I could fulfill a dream. And, Alex, who as of Wednesday of last week, was made, with free and clear title, co-owner of The Mangrove. This is the purpose of our celebration tonight, to acknowledge what has been true all along: I wouldn't be here without her. Billie wrapped Alex in her arms and hugged her. Then many in the group standing around them took their turn offering celebratory wishes to Alex and showing affection to both of them.

Twenty-Eight

Billie's celebration lasted until midnight. Jody, exhausted from the events of the weekend, departed about ten o'clock. All the guests had left and Billie, Alex and I put things away and locked the restaurant up for the night. I asked Billie and Alex to leave a door open for me, bid them good night and walked down Duval Street to a deserted Mallory Square. Despite the alcohol of the evening, and the stress of the weekend, I was not ready for sleep. My mind spun with the events of the past few days.

I leaned up against the railing at the water's edge. The wind coming off the Florida Straights was steady and refreshing. Humid air blurred the lights from Sunset Key across the bay. When my eyes adjusted to the darkness, I could see three sailboats anchored off shore. I bent over, rested my forearms on the railing and drew in a deep breath of salt air. I closed my eyes and relished the peace of the moment as I tried, but failed, to empty my mind. Like planets orbiting the sun, the events of the week circumnavigated my mind.

All through Billie's celebratory party, I couldn't get Helen Holland out of my mind. It wasn't the reunion of Helen and Jody that captured my thinking. It was the frailty of the mind, and the delicate balances of mind and body that create sanity. The causes of my depression were different from Helen's. A chemical imbalance in the brain created hers. Incorrect information planted in a young impressionable mind by my father had created mine. Either way, a departure from reality resulted. And in that altered state, Helen and I were both capable of unspeakable violence.

It struck me that mental health was delicate. Our psyche was so fragile, so easily shaped by others or modified by a few chemical molecules. I considered how precious mental health was and how thankful I was to be on the other side of my depression.

Helen's story was but a footnote compared to the tome I could write about Jody. When I analyzed the horrific circumstances of her youth and what a positive, warm and sensitive person had risen from the ashes of that destruction, I was in awe of her. She had enormous character. Wounded? Yes. Scarred? Yes. Still suffering from the ravages inflicted upon her? Yes. But in spite of circumstances that would have destroyed a lesser person, she thrived. She maintained her mental balance. This is the miracle of the story of Helen Holland. This indefatigable spirit of Jody's was the heart of any story I might write about her and her mother.

I should still be licking my wounds over Emily and Decker's impending nuptials. I should still be angry at the way they disrespected me. Some might even view my rapid repentance and forgiveness of Emily as premature or even naive. But I had stood next to Jody and glimpsed the enormity of the evil inflicted upon her. And I knew, when we sat with Helen for the first time, that Helen was right. The only way to let go was to forgive.

My issues with Emily seem petty. Yes, Decker and Emily's betrayal humbled me. It didn't compare to the humiliation Jody suffered at the hands of her mother. And what was Jody's response? She chose to face the issue. Standing in the light of such character, Emily's offense seemed insignificant.

I was optimistic.

I believed that Helen and Jody would work hard at reconciliation. Counseling would take time. But I knew Jody would rise above it. I knew my relationship with Emily would evolve. I looked forward to Billie's impending pregnancy, it was not without risks but she and Alex would face it together. And it was with enthusiasm that I considered my move to Key West.

The End

If you liked this Book.

Reviews are critical. Many paid promotional sites require a minimum number of "reviews" before they will allow an independent author to advertise. Without these sites, independent authors like me have little or no hope of gaining an audience for their work. If you liked this book, please leave a review. Eloquent words are not necessary. Even a simple, "I liked this book," would be helpful. If you feel compelled to say more, you have my gratitude.

Joe and the Governor, the Next Book in the *Jack McNamara Chronicles*.

Following "Contact Information" and "Bill Cronin's Other Books," we have included the first three chapters of *Joe and the Governor*, the fourth book in the *Jack McNamara Chronicles* series. This book can be pre-ordered now, and will be published July 15, 2016

Contact Information

For more information on Bill Cronin's novels, visit his website here.
http://billcroninwrite.com.

To receive updates and news on Bill Cronin's books, "like" his Facebook page here.
http://facebook.com/billcroninwrite.

You can contact the author directly here:
billcroninwrite@gmail.com

Bill Cronin's Other Books

Dial Tone, 2012
http://amzn.to/1QJtbph

The Song of the Mockingbird,
Book 1 Jack McNamara Chronicles, 2013
http://amzn.to/1QJsbuK

The Tainted Lady, 2014
http://amzn.to/1QJsFRr

Ruby's Story, Book 2 Jack McNamara Chronicles, 2014
http://amzn.to/1QJstBy

Joe and the Governor

Chapter 1

I've often stood on Whitehead Street across the road from Ernest Hemingway's Home and Museum and tried to imagine the scope of Hemingway's career. One of the most complex men ever to take a number-two lead pencil to paper, Hemingway wrote seven novels, six collections of short stories, two works of non-fiction and collected the Pulitzer and Nobel prizes. But my reason for gawking at his home had nothing to do with his inspiring career.

I wanted to understand what led Hemingway to buy this house. It wasn't a large structure. Even by the standards of 1931, it wasn't ostentatious. Why here? Why this particular spot? I was here in Key West to find a place of my own. I already knew I wanted something quiet and secluded. My home in Mount Dora, Florida had a separate, detached building I used as a studio that had suited my purposes. I was curious about Hemingway's and whether examining it would offer something I hadn't considered.

From my research, I knew of several reasons he selected Key West. First, the Florida Straights between Key West and Cuba was home to the best sport fishing in the world. Fishing drew Hemingway to Key West in 1928, a place to unwind from seven years as an ex-patriot in Paris. In 1931, he and his wife Pauline purchased the abandoned, neglected Whitehead Street mansion amid the great depression. They bought it for taxes owed—a mere eight-thousand dollars. For a perspective, if they had purchased the home today, they would have paid one-hundred-twenty-eight-thousand for property worth more than a million dollars. On just over an acre of ground, the location offered privacy. The three thousand square feet building was large enough to handle his growing family and provided space for frequent guests. Numerous French doors opened onto the wrap-around verandas on both floors. They provided adequate ventilation to combat Key West's stifling heat and humidity. While all these were positive considerations, what I think attracted Hemingway to this particular spot was the detached two-story building to the rear of the property. A garage took up the bottom floor. Tattered servant's quarters occupied the second, which he had converted to a studio. Hemingway needed a workroom away from distractions. At the time, he'd been writing the manuscript for Death in the Afternoon and a place to write, I thought, would've been foremost in his mind. In time, Hemingway had a bridge constructed from his second story veranda, near his bedroom, to the second story workroom above the garage.

As I stood and observed the Hemingway grounds, what stood out was an ill-constructed, six-foot high, redbrick wall. It surrounded the property on three sides. In 1935, Hemingway hired Toby Bruce, a family friend and woodworker from Piggott, Arkansas to build it. Having no experience as a bricklayer, Bruce's inexperience was evident in the meandering lines of the out-of-level bricks. A tour company in Key West had added Hemingway's abode to their circuit. Hemingway had built the wall to keep the curious from wandering about his yard. It took Bruce an entire summer to construct the barrier. While city leaders viewed the structure as an eyesore, Hemingway was well pleased. Bruce may have been a novice, but the wall still stands after more than sixty years and several hurricanes.

I hadn't considered a fence for security. In Mount Dora, FL, five hours to the north, my home sat on a lake in a suburban setting two miles from the city center. Not once, in all the years I'd lived and written there, did I have any issues with invasive tourists. When I compared my career to Hemingway's, the commercial success of my novels and movies had exceeded his. I'd written more novels, and my gross sales had been greater than his even adjusting for the differences in value of the dollar from the 1930s and 40s to 1996. Yet, even in the early stages of his career, he was such an icon he had to construct a wall to keep out curious fans. It was humbling. While my work had enjoyed commercial success, I knew nothing I'd written could compete with Hemingway's two literary prizes.

I'd been fortunate. I'd spent my life doing what I love to do; write novels. I had no pretentions about what I had written. I picked genre fiction and topics designed to appeal to the masses. While I'd considered writing a more literary work, the need to make a living predominated. In that endeavor, I had done well. I wanted to write a book like, The Old Man and the Sea, something noteworthy. I'd always been in awe of the simplicity of the subject matter of Hemingway's most praised work. But I had yet to find a subject whose theme rose to the level of compelling greatness. I'd just refreshed my contract with Reynolds & Ryan Publishing. I'd negotiated and received wider latitude in what I wrote, and they'd agreed to buy three non-genre books of my choosing. I'd hoped to pursue a topic of substance, a serious attempt at literature. The "what" had eluded me. As with so many of my books, the ideas for them often came in serendipitous fashion. My attempt at prize winning literature would have to wait. I had matters more pressing. I needed to decide if I was going to move to Key West. If I was serious about the move, I needed to find a home that met my needs.

Three months ago, following the completion of my last novel, I'd announced at a party thrown by my half-sister Billie that I'd intended to sell my house in Mount Dora and move to Key West. At the time, there were several factors pushing me in that direction. Then it seemed like a stellar idea. Standing across the street from Hemingway's, I was having second thoughts.

First, I'd just gone through a divorce after an eight-year marriage to Emily. A three-year writing dry spell caused by severe depression sent me to an emotional bottom. The spiral downward didn't wear well on Emily. Complicating matters, Emily was my manager and editor, a job she still held. During my bout with depression, Emily sought the solace of my best friend, Bob Decker, who was also going through a rough patch in his marriage. The mutual commiseration evolved into an affair, which Emily kept secret until the ink was dry on our divorce papers. Two weeks before she would marry Decker, she took me out to a public place and confessed her affair. She said she kept it a secret because she didn't think I was emotionally stable enough to handle such difficult news. She made it clear she liked working for me and wanted to continue in the role of manager and editor. At that point, I needed Emily's skills. While writing novels takes skill, the editing and revision process takes a mediocre work and transforms it into something noteworthy. She was more than a line or copy editor. She analyzed each draft for content, guiding my revisions and she drove me to raise the level of my writing. Emily and I were a good team. The work we produced was successful. Then, I was in no position to fire her. But I didn't have to be in the same town with her and Decker either. There were too many memories of Emily in my home in Mount Dora. Even though I still had to work with her, I didn't want to be around her.

Second, my half-sister Billie lived in Key West. Within the last year, we had reunited. I hadn't seen her in thirty years. She owned a restaurant in Key West, The Mangrove, on the corner of Duval Street and Olivia Street, a block from Hemingway's house. My father had just recently passed away while my divorce from Emily was in the process. Aside from my aunt Glory Jean, my mother's sister, who lived in Savannah, Billie was my only living relative. Following Emily's news, I needed that familial connection. When my depression reached rock bottom, I'd come to Key West to find my sister and to attempt to reconcile our relationship.

Third, when I was fourteen, Billie was instrumental in introducing me to Jody Holland, the first girl I ever kissed and loved. Tragedy struck Jody's family and cut our budding romance short in a disturbing way. At the same time, I was searching for Billie, Jody had moved to Key West and wandered into Billie's restaurant and recognized Billie immediately. They became instant friends. When I came to Key West looking for Billie, she reconnected me with Jody. It was Jody and Billie who helped me work my way out of my depression and put me on the road to writing again.

In the months following, my relationship with Emily imploded. Jody and I found the chemistry that drew us together as kids produced the same reaction more than thirty years later. I was in love with her and, as time progressed, it expanded and grew more comfortable. She owned a successful business in Key West and had deep roots there. If I wanted to be with her, I needed to make the move.

In light of all these factors, moving to Key West seemed natural. In fact, as I stood across from Hemingway's, I couldn't think of one rational reason for not making the move. Still, I was hesitant. Billie, Jody and I had emotional scars. We all had childhood events that had wounded us and had eaten away at the edges of our happiness. We'd built our emotional foundations on shifting sand.

Our mother abandoned Billie when she was a small child, and again when she was eighteen. It wasn't until Billie had met Alexandra that she'd been able to move past childhood events and stitch a meaningful life together.

In 1961, Jody's mother had suffered from postpartum psychosis and shot four of her brothers and sisters and her father. She'd shot Jody, too, but had only inflicted a grazing wound to her head. The courts committed Jody's mother to a mental institution where they incarcerated her for ten years. Three months ago, Jody and her mother reunited after thirty years. Jody's mother, Helen, was staying in Key West while she and Jody attended joint counseling to work through the emotional damage created so long ago.

We were all wounded souls. We were all needy. But it was my relationship with Jody that gave me pause. I had no idea how counseling would affect our relationship. I was hesitant to make such a huge life investment in Key West until I'd more time to see how my relationship with Jody worked out.

I dodged passing cars, crossed Whitehead Street and aimed down Olivia Street, walking past the crooked brick wall and past Hemingway's studio on my way to Billie's restaurant.

Behind The Mangrove, a driveway served as a pad for a dumpster and a place where trucks delivered food and supplies. There was a man dressed in soiled clothes sitting on a fruit crate. I wouldn't have taken notice except the restaurant hadn't opened yet, and he seemed out of place. As I walked past the drive, the man with an unshaven face looked up at me with clear blue eyes and smiled. I nodded and continued down to the corner of Duval Street and Olivia Street, turned right and approached the front gate. Billie had converted an old two-story home into a restaurant. The front yard of the house was a brick-paved, courtyard and outdoor dining area. Two towering banyan trees shaded it. The corner lot was bound by a white picket fence with an entry gate on Duval. At the entrance, a tall white, wooden podium served as a host station. A sign read, "Closed." I unlocked the gate and ambled past teak wood tables covered by forest green canvas umbrellas to the old home, which sat to the back of the lot.

Billie redesigned the house into a kitchen and indoor dining area. When you came through the front door, bathrooms were to the left, a café door to the kitchen was straight ahead and to the right a dining room that had been the living room of the large home. A stairway hugged the wall and led to a second floor, which provided storage and an office for Billie. Behind it, where the old dining room had been, Billie had converted it to a private dining area for large parties or meetings. Billie was in the kitchen, talking with her chef, Molly Flynn.

I'd just returned to Key West from Mount Dora the night before. I stayed at Billie's home last night, and she had invited me to have brunch with her this morning.

When I approached the café doors that separated the kitchen from the front door, Billie turned away from

Molly and looked at me. In contrast to her flyaway, rusty, red hair, her brilliant green eyes dominated her round face.

She pushed the doors apart, hugged me, stood back, looked at me and said, "You look rested. And warm! Look at you, you're dripping wet."

"I was standing in the sun looking over Hemingway's museum. It's a lot more humid in the middle of July than it was when I was here in April."

"They don't call it the mold capital for nothing. But, I love it. All the snowbirds are gone, and except for the cruise ships, we locals have the island all to ourselves."

"Before I forget it, when I was walking up Olivia, I noticed a man milling about behind your restaurant."

Billie led me into the empty dining room. They had set the table for two. We sat across from one another.

"It must be Joe. Homeless guy?"

I nodded.

"Joe and I have an arrangement. I let him pitch a tent in the back behind the dumpster in exchange for him keeping the yard picked up and keeping others from rummaging through my dumpster. We have a real homeless problem in Key West. People were going through my trash after I closed the restaurant. By itself, that wasn't a problem, but they were pulling garbage out of the dumpster and throwing it on the ground, leaving a mess. Joe offered to help."

"Do you pay him?"

"No. He won't take money from me. I offered to feed him but he won't have it. The only thing he wants is a safe place to sleep at night. The shelters are full, and the chances of finding a place where he won't be robbed or mugged are slim."

"So does he just hang around all day?"

"No. Not at all. He packs his belongings in the morning, puts them into a shed I have in the back and goes off for places unknown during the day. But here is the strange thing. One day a week, he gets all cleaned up, puts on clean clothes, comes into the restaurant through the front gate and has a meal, like a regular customer. He insists on paying the bill. And he leaves a generous tip for the servers."

"What do you know about him?"

"Nothing. He never talks about himself. He deflects every personal question I ask him. But, Jack, he's one of the most intelligent people I've ever talked to. He's a mystery, that one. Every time I talk to him, I think about you. He seems like an awesome character for a book. You should meet him—talk to him."

"I'd like that."

Like I said. Sometimes ideas for stories come to you in serendipitous ways.

Joe and the Governor
Chapter 2

When I'd arrived late last night, Billie and Alex had already gone to bed. Billie left the back door unlocked and I'd gone up to her guest room. Both Billie and Alex had already gone before I got up.

The chef brought us eggs benedict, a plate of cantaloupe to share and a decanter of coffee.

Once we settled into our meal I asked, "So tell me, how's In-Vitro going?"

When I was here in April, Billie announced she and Alex were going to try to have a baby. Billie, in her early fifties, had already gone through menopause, but she wanted to carry the baby. IVF was their only option. Billie had already been to see a fertility doctor in Miami for an initial consultation when I was here last.

"The clinic performed all the tests. The docs gave me a green light. The biggest snag is a legal one. Using eggs and sperm from donors is more complicated than I thought. It is almost like a legal adoption, where the donors agree to give up legal ownership and custody of their eggs and sperm. We're all set to go, procedure wise. I just want to meet with Cynthia before I sign all the papers. I want to understand what I'm getting into."

Cynthia Pike was her attorney and friend.

"Sounds complicated." When she told me she was considering IVF, I'd never thought about the legal issues.

"The fertility clinic says it isn't complicated. All the sperm and egg donors sign forms and give up all their rights of custody. We have to file court papers to become legal parents of the fertilized eggs or embryos. But the docs want me to sign a form that holds them harmless if at some point the egg or sperm donors want to sue for custody. Sometimes, that can happen. Alex and I felt like we needed Cynthia to go over all this with us before we press ahead."

"What kind of tests did they have to do?"

"They had to determine if I was healthy enough to carry a baby for nine months. I'm fifty-two, Jack. I'm no spring chicken. They had to examine all my female plumbing and perform a mock embryo transfer, which is too personal to go into detail. But they just want to make sure they don't encounter any issues during the procedure.

"After the legal issues, Alex and I have some tough decisions. For example, the most important decision is how many embryos do we want to implant?"

"I don't understand. Why would you consider more than one?"

"Jack, they drain your bank account every time they perform this procedure. Implanting more than one embryo increases the chances of a successful pregnancy. But it also means I could have twins or triplets depending on the number of embryos we choose to implant."

"Doesn't that increase the risk of health complications?"

"Yes, but the fertility docs assure me I'm healthy enough to handle a multiple pregnancy."

"Are you and Alex prepared for something like that? I mean, you have this restaurant to take care of. Could you handle the stress of more than one child?"

"I don't know, Jack. Alex and I are working through that now. I think I'm more concerned about the prospect of not having a child. This is very important to me." Billie gave emphasis to the word "very." "I want to be able to give a youngster the childhood I never had. This is about me, as much as it is about having a baby."

When I thought about the loveless childhood Billie had had, abandoned by my mother as a toddler and abandoned by her uncaring natural father, I could empathize. This would mean she would have a teenage child when she was in her late sixties. I wanted to raise it as an issue for her to consider, but thought better of it.

"So how is Alex feeling about this? She was against this, wasn't she?"

"Yes. You helped us work through it, Jack, and I appreciate it. After you left here in April, Alex and I went to see my doctors. When they explained to Alex the tests they would do to insure I was healthy enough for the procedure, it alleviated her concerns. Now that the docs have done all the exams, she's good. The legal issues are another matter. She's troubled about the problems that could come up. Our meeting with Cynthia is pretty important."

"So what comes next?"

"It's a simple process for me, since I'm using donated eggs and sperm. I go into the doctor's office, and they inject embryos into my uterus. This is nothing more than might happen in a routine pelvic exam. If I were younger, and using my own eggs, the docs would treat me with synthetic hormones to stimulate the ovaries to produce more than one egg. After fourteen days, they'd give me more medication to help the eggs mature. I would receive more medications to prevent the body from releasing the developed eggs too soon. Whether a woman uses her own eggs, or donated eggs, they give you progesterone supplements to make the lining of the uterus more receptive to implantation.

"If I'd been using my own eggs, the Doc would retrieve them. From that point on, the procedure is the same whether I have eggs or use a donor. First, the clinic would fertilize the egg. After about six days, they perform genetic tests to ensure the embryo is healthy and there are no birth defects. The Doc implants the embryo and checks the progress of the pregnancy. Of course, there's no assurance I'll get pregnant on the first try. Although the fertility clinic plays up their success rate, they also are honest that they may have to make several attempts before I get pregnant. Because of my age, the chances of more than one attempt are higher, and there's more of a risk of delivering a pre-mature baby, or in the worst case, I have a miscarriage. They'll give me medications to prevent this, but there's still that chance."

"When do you meet with Pike?"

"We meet in a day or two when Alex returns. I was hoping you'd come with Alex and me. I'd like you to be there. You may think of something to ask her Alex and I haven't thought of."

"I'm concerned about being a fifth-wheel with Alex."

"Alex suggested it, Jack."

"I appreciate you wanting to include me, but this is personal, Billie. This is something you and Alex should do."

We chatted while we ate and finished our meal. We refilled our coffee cups.

Billie asked, "Did you put your house up for sale in Mount Dora?"

"No. I know I said I was going to do that, but I decided I'd hold off for now."

"Getting cold feet about moving here, Jack?"

"No, not yet anyway. I thought it might be wise to try to find a place first and live here a while before I severed ties with Central Florida. Homes are so expensive here, I'm wondering whether it would be wise to rent before I buy."

"Tell me about it. I bought our house through a foreclosure sale. Today the taxable value is over a million and the taxes are killing us. We paid half that amount just six years ago. The problem is land to build new homes is scarce. Because of a shortage of water and sewer facilities in the keys, the government limits building permits. Jody paid more for her little cracker house than Alex and I paid for ours. It's nuts."

"It's hot in the summer in Mount Dora, but nothing compared to the heat and humidity you have here."

"For six months, it's paradise here. And we're currently in the wrong six months."

"Yeah, and then the Conch Republic morphs into hell on earth."

"Thank God for the cruise ships or we would starve. So what kind of a house are you looking for? You know you're welcome to stay at our house as long as you like. And Jody would be ecstatic if you moved in with her."

"I'm not ready for that yet, Billie. Besides, what I need is a place to write that's free of distractions."

"You're welcome to one of our bedrooms. We have three that just collect dust."

"I appreciate your offer, but in Mount Dora, I have a separate building for my studio. The previous owners had it built as a guesthouse with its own kitchenette and bath. I need something like that, here. And it needs to be private and quiet."

"And my house won't do?"

"Interruptions and distractions are the kiss of death to a writer. As good as my focus and concentration skills are, I need seclusion. All Mrs. Berger would have to do is fire up the vacuum cleaner she runs twice a week and she'd ruin my day of writing."

"She's not the quietest person on the planet."

"And Jody's place is just too small. There's no place to write except on her back patio, and there's too much ambient noise there."

"If you're looking for something on the Island to buy, that could be expensive."

"With real estate prices going up so quick here, it sounds like a good place to invest."

"But you're hesitant. I thought you wanted to get away from Emily. She's still working for you isn't she?"

"For now. I do want to get away from her. It's just too close, especially with her married to my best friend. The problem isn't just the house in Mount Dora. She still works for me. Before I can do anything about that, I need to find another editor and manager. And I don't want to do anything until I make up my mind about Key West."

"I thought you decided to move here. It's Jody isn't it? You're not sure about Jody?"

"Jody needs space right now, Billie. She has her mother here, they're in counseling right now and, well, there's no telling how all this will affect her."

"I think you're wrong about her needing space. While you've been away, she's been missing you something awful. The woman is in love, Jack. She needs you. All this turmoil with her mom has dredged up long suppressed feelings. She's struggling."

"I know Billie. I talk to her everyday on the phone. And it's upsetting to listen to her go through it."

"Is that what's bothering you?"

"I don't know. I want to help her, but what can I do? I feel helpless."

"You still feel the same about her?"

"Yes."

"I think all she needs right now is you to be there for her. I don't think she wants or needs anything but your love and support."

"I know."

"She's anxious to see you, too. I think she was a little disappointed about not having breakfast with us."

"She was a little upset I didn't stay with her last night."

"Something's going on Jack. What is it?"

"Billie, I've just recovered from a significant depression of my own. No sooner do I have my life back together; my publisher fires me. Emily divorces me, my father passes away and I find out Emily had been having an affair with my best friend. On top of that, Jody and I went digging into her past, the reunion with her mother and it's all a little much. I'm hesitant to wade into another emotional quagmire."

"We haven't mentioned all my junk; almost losing my restaurant and issues over having a child."

"It isn't that Billie. It is the sum of all of it. I needed a break."

"Is that why it took you three months to return to the Keys?

"Part of the reason . . . okay, yes it was the reason."

"Then why are you thinking about a move here?" There was a wounded quality to Billie's voice. A sarcastic tone.

"For starters, I love you. You're pretty much the only family I have. And I'm in love with Jody. I want to be here."

"I don't want to be a burden to you, Jack."

I regretted the turn in our conversation. "Billie, you're misunderstanding me."

Billie lifted her elbows off the table and pushed back into her chair. "Doesn't sound like it to me."

"You aren't my concern, Billie. I'm not worried about you. It's Jody. She's looking for a commitment from me, one I'm unwilling to make until I see how everything goes with her mother."

"I thought you saw Jody and her mother going through counseling as a positive step."

"It is."

"You said you admired her courage and wisdom in hitting her issues with her mother head on."

"Yes, I did. And I still feel that way. I do admire her. It demonstrates a lot of character. But I guarantee the process she's going through with her mother will change her."

"Yes, there could be changes. But do you think that part of Jody, the part you fell in love with as a boy and now again after all these years as a man, will have changed? She's one of the finest people I've ever known and she's in love with you. Yes, she's dealing with some significant emotional issues. You can't experience what she went through without collateral damage. But, she's dealing with it, facing it. You were a mess when you first came to Key West, and Jody jumped in that hole you were in and helped you dig yourself out. She didn't hesitate."

"I know, Billie. I know. I'm grateful to her and to you. You both saved my life. And I'm not having second thoughts about her. I just want to go slow. I just want to make sure it's a relationship that can endure."

"It's endured for over thirty years, Jack. I don't know how much more enduring it can be."

"You're right." I threw up my hands. "You're right. I'm worrying for nothing."

"You should go find, Jody. But, tonight's the night Joe usually comes and has dinner. There're no ships in town, so tonight will be slow. Why don't you and Jody come and have dinner with me. I want you to meet this guy."

I agreed.

Joe and the Governor

Chapter 3

Ninety degrees plus ninety percent humidity equal miserable. Even though I'd dressed for the heat in shorts, a light T-shirt and flip-flops, my clothes stuck to my skin. Jody's art gallery was halfway down Duval Street between Billie's restaurant and the Pier House. It was nearing noon, and the foot traffic on the sidewalk was light. The smell of the sea filled the air. The sun was relentless and shade elusive.

The Pegasus Art Gallery logo in gold leaf was emblazoned on the glass entry door. Jody had filled the plate glass window with several watercolors featuring a local artist. An electronic bell chimed as I opened the door to enter. Jody was sitting behind a small table that doubled as a stand for her cash register and a work surface. She looked up from her work, saw it was me, bolted from the chair, crossed the short distance between us and threw her arms around me. I returned her hug with enthusiasm. She kissed me on the mouth.

"Mmmmm, have I missed those." And she kissed me again, longer and deeper. She pulled back. "Yes, indeed I have." Her eyes beamed; a smile spread across her thin face.

"You look marvelous, Jody." And she did. As I was holding her, the conversation I'd just had about commitment with Billie echoed. In her arms, those feelings seemed silly and melted away. I pulled away from her. "I'm soaked. I'm going to mess up your clothes. And I smell like last year's laundry."

"We need to get you out of those clothes, then." She winked at me. "I think we should close up for lunch, go to my house, and we'll run your clothes through the dryer. And maybe while we're waiting we can think of something to do. A shower perhaps?"

And that's what we did. Afterwards, we sat on her small deck behind her conch-style house and she and I caught up. The lunch-hour stretched into two hours.

I asked her, "Don't you need to get back to the gallery?"

"Okay. Let me see. I haven't seen you in three months. You're in my house and you're sitting on my porch. I was thinking that as soon as we finish our lemonade, we could find our way back to my bed. So why would I want to go back to the gallery? Unless of course you want me to go?"

I smiled at her. This was typical Jody, a playful, unabashed tease.

We spent the afternoon, napping, playing and catching up. An hour before dusk, we dressed and walked the short distance to the Pier House sunset deck. We selected a table with an unobstructed view of the setting sun. We ordered Margaritas and then sat close together watching silhouetted boats of every description motor past the deck.

Jody volunteered. "My mother and I are meeting twice a week now."

I'd wanted to ask how the counseling sessions were going with her mother. I'd learned with Jody, on this particular subject, it was best not to pry. Over the past three months, we'd talked on the phone every day. I took the position that when she was ready to talk about her mother, she would. It had been a couple of weeks since she'd brought the topic up. She'd already told me a month ago they'd increased their joint counseling sessions to twice a week.

"Oh? How is that going?"

"If Dr. Carnes asks me one more time about how I feel about something, I'm going to scream."

"So, how are you feeling about all this?" I drew out the word feeling and smiled.

Jody punched me on the arm.

I asked, "Has it accomplished anything?"

"When we started meeting with Dr. Carnes, I'd no idea what to expect. In our first meeting, Dr. Carnes asked my mother to share what was in her heart. That took up the entire first session."

"What did she say?"

"Same thing she told us when we first met with her. She knows what she did was wrong; she was out of her mind when she did it. While she feels horrible about what happened, she's adamant it was not her fault."

"Your reaction?"

"Mentally, I understand it. I know she was sick. I understand it in my mind. Deep down, all I feel is rage. And, after three months of counseling, I still feel that way."

"Has there been any progress?"

"Yes. I can be in the same room with her. And our sessions are more like guided conversations. I know this is going to sound strange, but I'm beginning to see the anger I feel isn't connected to her. I'm beginning to see her as a person instead of a convenient bull's eye for my angst. The rage I feel is much broader than my mother. I haven't said this to Dr. Carnes, but I can separate my mother from that anger."

"How?"

"First, I understand the anger problem is my issue, not my mother's. She was the catalyst, the first-mover. My anger comes from my inability to deal with what happened to my family, not my mother. My anger goes beyond her."

"So who's the target of your anger?"

"I don't know, Jack. I'm still trying to sort it out. When we first met with my mother, she equated the tragedy of our family to a natural disaster. Hurricane Andrew was the example she used that stuck with me. I remember my anger as I watched the news coverage of the people that monster storm had killed. I remember the anger I felt that something so horrible and senseless could happen to the innocent."

"You know, Jody. I remember reacting the same way."

"Good. Now magnify that a hundred times and you approach how I'm feeling." Jody drew out the word feeling for emphasis.

"So you're angry at God?"

"Yes . . . No . . . I don't know. I'm angry at what I don't understand. But I agree with what my mother said to us three months ago. Tragedies occur all the time. Fate takes the lives of the innocent. And there's no one left standing to take the blame. I want someone to be responsible. I want to hurl my anger at someone. I want to hurt someone over what happened to my family. When I look at my mother, and what she's been through, I know she's not to blame. She was a victim, too."

"Sounds like a lot of progress to me."

"I suppose. A mixture of good and bad. The good news for my mother is she gets the target taken off her chest. The bad news is I don't know where to place the blame. I still have the anger. My life was simple before we started counseling. I hated my mother for what she did. Now it isn't simple any more. Now I still have the anger, but I don't know where to direct it. Here is the interesting part, Jack. I don't want to give up that anger. It has become a part of me. And while I may be able to forgive my mother, I'm concerned my desire to protect and sustain my anger is the real monster hiding under the bed."

"It seems to me your recognition of the problem is more than half the battle. Have you shared any of this in counseling?"

"No. I wanted to talk to you about it in person, first. I'll be honest. When I make that confession, and let my mother off the hook, the dynamics of the counseling will shift its focus to my issues. Do you remember the first time we met with my mother, we had this little exchange about why she wanted to see me. I assumed she wanted my forgiveness. If you recall, she said she didn't want or need my pardon. She had come to help me deal with the emotional damage created by what she'd done. I understand that now. She's not my problem and my mother has known it all along. My issue is that I haven't dealt with what happened to me in the correct way. The irony is I have an emotional illness that's the cause of my angst, not my mother. Once I let the cat out of the bag, I'll have Dr. Carnes and my mother pressing me to deal with it. The focus moves off my mother and what she did, to me."

"And how do you feel about that?" I again drug out the word feel into three or four syllables, and feigned a broad smile.

"I feeeeel like Dr. Carnes and my mom have me hog tied and they're dragging me toward mental health. I know I need to do this; everything in me is fighting against it. Do you think I'm crazy, Jack?"

"Quite the opposite. Even on my best days during my long bout with depression, I was not thinking as clearly as you are. I'm so impressed with your analysis and the conclusions you're coming to. You've a keen intelligence I find attractive."

"Thanks, you're kind to say that. But right now I don't feel like I have it together. So . . . you're only attracted to my intellect?" A hint of a smile broke at the corners of her mouth.

I said, "So you think what we did this afternoon was a meeting of the minds."

"Yeah, something like that." Her light brown eyes sparkled.

"Have you and your mother gotten together outside of counseling since I left for Mount Dora?"

"No. She's invited me several times to have a meal with her, but I declined. Until I'd sorted out my relationship with her, I didn't want to add any complications. I told her you were coming into town and she suggested you and I get together with her. She likes you, Jack. She always has."

"So you're okay with that?"

"If you're with me, yes. I think I'm ready. I need to share all this with her and Dr. Carnes tomorrow when we get together. I'll suggest we get together at Billie's for dinner. I'm not ready to invite her to my house."

"Billie wants us to come to dinner tonight. She wants me to meet this homeless guy named Joe."

"Billie has been talking about this guy for a couple of weeks now. I've seen him hanging around the restaurant."

"He gets cleaned up once a week and becomes a paying customer. Billie thinks this guy would be a good character for one of my books."

"Billie has an enormous heart, Jack. I just hope she knows what she's getting into."